COLD IRON

A CACHE IRON MYSTERY

ALEX BLAKELY

COPYRIGHT

This book is a work of fiction. The characters, incidents, and dialogue are drawn from the authors imagination and are not to be construed as real. Any resemblance to actual events or persons, living or dead, is entirely coincidental.

Kinclond Publishing Incorporated

P.O. Box 31, Milton, Ontario, Canada L9T 2Y3

https://kinclondpublishing.com

First ebook edition: March 2021

eISBN: 978-1-7773627-6-8

ISBN: 978-1-7773627-7-5

SNOW IN PARADISE

ache Iron looked out at the crystal-blue ocean waters; she had made it to one of the Italian beaches she wanted to visit most. The intense heat of the sun on that day caused perspiration to roll down the front of her neck and flow like a river through a canyon, congregating at the tip of her nipples. Drops of it would fall toward the sand below, evaporating before they hit the ground. The scent of coconut suntan lotion filled the air as people covered themselves everywhere to protect themselves from the intensity of the sun's rays. She had made it to one of the locations on the bucket list she had drafted after being stationed in Italy. Wearing only a pair of bikini bottoms and flip-flops, she looked at all the naked bodies scattered on the beach; reaching down to the sides of her bikini, she untied the straps, allowing them to fall on her flip-flops. Sixties-style music came from someone's radio as laughter and voices surrounded her. She preferred to tie her long brunette hair in a ponytail when she was off duty. Her five-foot-eight-inch athletic frame caught more than a few stares from gentlemen hiding their eyes behind mirrored shades as she found her ideal location on the beach to drop everything, including her towel. She scanned the beach. The occupants of the white sand were older men and women in their birthday suits, young girls playing catch in the buff and a few lifeguards trying to manage the show that day. One particular lifeguard captured Cache's attention, sitting up in a white wooden chair, its paint peeling at the base, weathered by the salty ocean air. His blond hair and chiseled abs caught her attention. She stood there in silence and pondered what her opening line should be. Someone called out her name, breaking the quiet.

"Cache, Cache, Ms. Iron, are you there?"

Cache looked in the voice's direction. The hot sand had turned to a deep blanket of Montana snow as the icy winds from the blizzard that had engulfed the ranch that afternoon ripped across what little bare skin she'd exposed to the elements, causing a burning sensation on her skin.

"Did I lose you?" her brother Cooper asked.

"I was just remembering somewhere warmer."

"Let's get this fence mended and we can head back to the house. Daddy will have a roaring fire going."

They worked for the next hour as the storm moved around them. Their well-protected ears could still hear the wind's moan. "You're not welcome out here this day," the winds said. They repaired a section of fence on the family cattle ranch and jumped on a snowmobile to race back to the ranch house, where the warmth of family and fire would wait for them.

They wandered into the log-frame house built by Irons several generations ago. Cache's father, Thomas Iron, sat on the couch listening to the radio as their dog, Duke, lay at his feet. The sounds of clanking came from the area of the kitchen as Cache's mother, Julie, worked to put some food together to serve her two children.

"Hey, what are they saying about the storm, Daddy? Have they given any updates?" Cache asked.

Her father motioned with his hand for her to quiet down as he played with the knob to turn up the volume. The radio announcer advised that a prison break had happened earlier that day as two prisoners were being transported from the prison in Quinn, Montana, to the state penitentiary in Deer Lodge. Reports were incomplete, given the storm, but they were advising the public to be on the lookout for Terry Bolden—age thirty-seven, six foot one, tall, muscular build, blond hair, buzz cut with multiple tattoos, including several on his neck—and his younger brother Leo Bolden, age thirty-three, five foot four with black hair, no visible tattoos. Police advised that anyone seeing someone who resembled either of these two men should not engage them but should call the police. They were likely armed and considered dangerous.

Cooper walked over to the window to look at the blowing snow, which was coming down thick enough that the barn was almost invisible, with only a hint of light coming from the lamp that sat above the barn doors. Cache's mom walked into the family room and put down two plates of food for them.

"You must be hungry, sit down and get something to eat," she said.

"I don't know, Mom, I think I might head home," Cooper said. "Beth is alone, and with criminals on the loose I might feel better being there."

Cache's father interjected, "Your brother Tommy is at home and is just across the laneway from her. If they are wise, they would stay clear of your brother."

"Not everyone knows Tommy, Dad, and two armed criminals with not much to lose would give him some trouble," Cooper said.

"That does it, I'm heading home. Sorry, Mom, it looks delicious," Cooper said.

"Well, you can wait a few minutes, I will wrap this up and you can take it with you."

Julie walked back to the kitchen to wrap dinner up for Cooper. Cache walked over to her older brother and put her head on his shoulder.

"I don't blame you. If I had someone to love out there in this, I would be itching to get back to them too."

"Don't worry about that, you'll find someone; he's out there somewhere."

Cache kissed her brother on the cheek as her mom brought Cooper a plastic container with his meal inside. As he opened the door and stepped outside into the freezing night air, he could hear his dad shout, "Close the door!" Cache watched from the family room window as he made it to his truck and then headed down the driveway. Cache turned to her parents. "Lucky he doesn't have far to go."

The house that Cache's parents called home had been the family residence for multiple generations of Irons on the Iron and Sons ranch. When Cache's grandfather had passed away, her parents had moved into the main house, vacating a smaller home on the property, which passed to the eldest brother, Tommy. Cooper and he had built a similar-sized house next to Tommy's when Cooper and Beth got married. Cache had spent most of her life in the main house except for when she went away to school or was in the service. She sat down on the big brown corduroy couch with her father on one end, trying to balance her dinner on her knees.

"Do you think they'll survive out in this storm, Daddy?"

"I don't know; this is bad. I don't think we've seen one this bad since the winter of '94. That one went on for a week. Lost about fifteen percent of the herd, damage to the barn and other buildings. Don't think I would want to be out on foot in this storm."

"Did the news say they were on foot?" Cache asked.

"They've said little, other than there are two escaped prisoners. I suspect most news people don't want to venture out into this weather. I'm sure the police will have everything well in hand. Still, I think we might want to take a rifle with us to bed tonight just in case they happen upon these parts."

Cache's mother had sat down in an overstuffed chair beside the fireplace. "They didn't say they were around here, did they, Tom?"

"They didn't say where they escaped, but given where Quinn is and where Deer Lodge is, the most direct route takes them past Hart, which means it's possible that they could be in the area. Cache, let's make sure everything is good and tight before we head for bed this evening. Did you and Cooper secure the barn before you came up to the house?"

"Yep, we put the snowmobile in the back shed and checked on the horses. Everything is secure down there; I don't foresee a reason we would need to venture out into the storm until morning." Tapping sounds came from the windows as freezing rain coated the glass with a thick sheet of ice. Winds howled outside like wolves calling out to their pack deep in the forest.

"Did you get the fence mended while you were out?"

"We had to string about twenty feet of new wire, but it should hold."

"Do you figure that we lost any cattle because of it?"

"Hard to say, but we'll need to survey the area once the storm lets up."

Cache's mother cleared her throat. "On a different topic, Cache, have you considered the offer from the community college to teach art history?"

"Hadn't thought much about it; Daddy needs me here on the ranch and I don't know if it's right for me."

"Don't let me be the excuse you don't pursue something. After all, I have your brothers to help me here on the ranch."

"So you're saying you don't need me?"

"Your brothers didn't go off to college to study art; it seems to me that it would be a poor investment, if you didn't do something with it."

"Honey, you went to Dartmouth for a reason, and it wasn't ranching; you joined the military, and it had nothing to do with ranching. I assume you're trying to find where you fit in the world."

"Isn't that what everyone is trying to do?"

"Yes, but not everyone is my daughter. Look, you want to ranch, then ranch; lord knows those boys need direction," Julie said.

"Hey, who do you think runs this place?" Tom said.

"Tom the boys need guidance and we won't always be here. I'm just saying that since you got home from the army, Cache, you seem lost, like you're going through the motions with no proper sense of direction."

Cache's father pointed his finger at Cache. "I have told you the same thing. You need to find direction. I don't know why you left the army; you traveled, it gave you a sense of purpose, you may have had a brilliant career there," Tom said.

"After six years, the fit wasn't there for me anymore; I grew restless. I need to do something else."

"Which is . . . ?" Julie asked.

"I don't know, I just figured I would come home and figure it out."

"Julie Cache Iron, you're a thirty-four-year-old woman living in your parents' home. At least your brothers have moved out."

"Pauly still lives here," Cache said.

"Pauly is still in his twenties, and when he passes thirty, I expect him to have moved out, found a nice young girl, and be working on giving me some more grandkids."

"Is this what this is about? You want me to have some guy knock me up so you can have some grandkids?" Cache asked.

"Don't you talk to your mother that way," Thomas said. "Look, kids, no kids, that is your choice. All we're saying is keep your options open. Want to be a rancher, then great, but do both. Teach part of the day and ranch the other part of the day. Honey, don't let the door close on you. I'm just afraid you'll look back on this in a few years as the opportunity that got away."

Cache let out a heavy sigh. "All right, I'll consider it." She rose from the couch and took her dishes to the kitchen. She returned to the family room, headed for the gun cabinet to retrieve her rifle, and said good night to her parents and her dog. As she climbed the stairs, she could hear her parents continuing to discuss her lack of direction. She felt like yelling out *I can hear you* to them, but she knew they already knew that.

In her room, Cache turned on a small lamp that sat on the end table closest to her bed and leaned her rifle up in the corner. Her bedroom still had posters of the rock bands she'd followed in her youth, with photographs taken while she was away at college and overseas taped on top of the posters. She flopped down on the bed and stared at the ceiling. The door popped open as her black Labrador Duke made his way into her room, jumping up on the bed and putting his head on her chest. She stroked his head and asked him, "What am I going to do with my life?" No surprise, there was no answer, just a pair of black eyes looking up at her and a wagging tail as he got his ears rubbed. She fell asleep with his warm body pressed against hers.

———

Cache woke around six thirty in the morning. She tried to look out the small bedroom window and couldn't see a thing. Her window was coated with ice, and snow clung to the window frame, providing no visibility. Winds continued to scream outside as she pulled on a washed pair of jeans and made her way downstairs to the kitchen. The smell of fresh-brewed coffee carried through the house, and as she neared the entrance to the kitchen, she could hear bacon sizzling in the frying pan.

"Good morning," Cache said.

"Good morning, dear, how did you sleep?" her mother asked.

"Well, Duke kept me warm," she said as she walked over to the coffeepot and poured herself a mug of coffee, and returned to sit down at the kitchen table. "Did Daddy go outside?"

Tom wandered into the kitchen. "No, Daddy didn't go out in that. Do you assume Daddy is dumb?" he said, making a silly face at his wife and daughter.

Tom sat down at the table as Cache's mother served them both eggs and bacon with a side of brown toast.

"Any news?" Cache's mother asked.

"About what?" Cache said.

"Oh, I was listening for updates on the escaped prisoners to see if the police had caught them, but they keep giving us the same warning with very few details about what happened and where it happened."

"Maybe they froze to death and that will be the end of them," Cache said.

The ring of the telephone interrupted the breakfast conversation. Tom rose from the kitchen table while Cache's mother urged him to let it ring and sit back down. Tom turned to her and said, "Could be one of the boys, maybe there's some trouble." He walked into the family room and picked up the phone. Cache and her mother listened in on the conversation to determine what the call was all about.

"Hello? . . . Yes, this is he. . . . Mason, hey, it's been a while, how are you and Mabel, you okay? . . . Well, what can I do for you? . . . No, I have my hands full with the ranch, why do you ask? . . . Yeah, I found out about it over the radio, they're not saying much. Why, have you discovered something more? . . . Saugeen Mountain, that's close to us, about ninety minutes north of Hart. . . . Every morning I get an unfamiliar ache in a place I never had an ache before. . . . That's not bad pay for showing some officers the backcountry, but I don't think it's for me. . . . Um, you know, I might have someone in mind, very experienced in the backcountry, knows how to handle themselves. . . . It's actually she, my daughter, Cache. Grew up on the ranch, knows the backcountry, army trained. I will have to check with her first. . . . Let me talk to her and I'll ask her to get back to you either way. . . . Hey, thanks, Mason, for calling. . . . Yeah, we'll talk later."

Cache could hear her father hang up the phone and

make his way back to the kitchen. He shared with Cache and her mother that the caller was Mason Riggs, a local rancher who had served as a guide to the backcountry to local law enforcement over the years when they needed help. Her father explained that the law enforcement detachment out of Quinn was organizing a group of officers to venture up toward Saugeen Mountain as they looked for the escaped prisoners and needed a guide familiar with the terrain. Given Mason's age, he'd declined their request and recommended him to the police.

"What about you, are you interested?" he asked Cache.

"She is not, Tom Iron, how foolish can you be?" her mother said.

"Why don't we let her speak for herself."

Cache just smirked and reflected on it for a minute. "What does it pay?" she asked.

"Mason said they're offering two hundred and fifty dollars a day."

"That's good money to show some people around. However, I'm not sure this weather is something that we should venture out in."

"Cache, are you crazy, going after escaped prisoners? You might get hurt or worse."

"Mom, I was in the army, I think I have had to deal with a lot worse than two escaped prisoners."

Tom said, "Consider it, but they're planning on heading out today, guide or no guide."

"Sounds like they'll need the help."

"Without an experienced guide, a few good people might lose their lives."

"You always said we should help those in need."

"Our family always has, but you have to decide if this is right for you."

Cache got up from the kitchen table, walked into the family room with her cup of coffee, and sat down to ponder the situation. She could hear angry whispers coming from the kitchen, and she knew her mother would be extra worried if she ventured out there. She sipped her coffee and thought about how best to handle the situation. Given the weather, the officers might need to seek shelter out there.

"Dad, Dad, can you come here for a second?"

"Yeah, what?"

"Who do we know who has a hunting lodge up near Saugeen?"

A smile came over her dad's face. "Henderson, Shellington, and Myers all have places up that way, about twenty miles apart."

"If we head up that way, I'll need to check with them to see if it's okay for us to use their places if we need shelter."

"Are you going to take the job?"

"I can offer my services; worst thing they can say is no thank you."

With that, Cache called Mason Riggs back and expressed her interest in helping. Mason would contact the sergeant organizing the group and pass on her information. They talked for a few minutes longer as Cache picked his brain to take full advantage of his knowledge of the area. "I have explored the area before," she said. "If I remember correctly, as you move up the mountain there are some nasty drop-off points."

"Yeah, and that's what you'll need to be vigilant about. In the summer, when the snow isn't present, they're easier to identify, but you could step onto to an area that might prove detrimental, like walking on thin ice."

"They're not marked at all?"

"Nah, most people don't venture into those areas this

time of the year, and keep in mind with this storm your visibility could be an issue. Also, don't put too heavy a reliance on electronic devices; not sure whether you'll get a strong GPS signal in this storm."

"Yeah, I tend to navigate with compass and map."

"I will pass your info on to the sergeant in charge; his last name is Malone. If you head out with them and get stuck at all, call me if you have reception, I'll give you my input as best as I can."

"If I don't have a signal?"

"Then do what the army trained you to do. Talk to you later."

With that, Cache hung up the phone and wandered back into the kitchen. She went to her mother and gave her a hug to assure her that everything would be all right. All they could do was wait and see if the officers had any interest in her joining their team. Cache went upstairs and pulled supplies together into her backpack in the event they called her. She packed thermal clothing, a knife, a small foldout saw, a first-aid kit, food supplies, a flare gun, fire-starter fuel and ammunition for her rifle and handgun. She put the pack at the foot of her bed, lay back down and thought about what it would be like to be on a manhunt again. Over the six years she'd been with the service, a few times she'd encountered people trying to evade the military police and she'd had to help track them down.

2

HIRE AN IRON

An hour had passed since Cache had spoken to Mason. She had an uneasiness sitting in her stomach that she'd had before. Over the years she'd felt she needed to go farther than her male counterparts to show that she was more than capable and worried that the fact that she was a woman might hinder the police from considering her for the job. The storm raged outside, and most people with any common sense would have waited inside until it blew over, but the manhunt was calling her; she could feel it. The one thing she missed most from her days in the military was the adrenaline rush that would come when she needed to be her best to end a dangerous situation and protect herself and her comrades. She yearned for that excitement again. Her decision to leave the military had not been an easy one. She had felt that she needed to come home to prove to her father she was just as capable of running the ranch as her brothers. Yet life on the ranch was more tame than what she had become used to.

She was listening as the freezing rain pounded the small

window in her bedroom when in the distance, she could hear the phone ring.

"Cache, it's for you."

Cache leaped off her bed and flew down the stairs, missing two steps and almost tumbling down the rest. She grabbed the phone from her father, covering the mouthpiece with her hand, to catch her breath, so she didn't sound like a groupie about to talk to her favorite band on a radio station.

"Hello, Cache Iron here."

"Ms. Iron, my name is Angelo Malone, I'm a sergeant with the Quinn Police Department. Mason Riggs passed your name on to me with his recommendation. He said you would be the right person for us."

"Yeah, I'm interested in helping you out if you need a guide."

"That is great, but I think I have to be square with you before you sign on."

"Okay."

"So, I don't know if you've been following the news. We have two prisoners who escaped from transport. They were being moved from the prison in Quinn to the state penitentiary in Deer Lodge."

"Yeah, we learned about it on the radio."

"So, the two men we are looking for are Terry and Leo Bolden. It's important that you know that we suspect them in the disappearance and killing of several women. The state couldn't make the case against them on those charges and they never went to trial for the murders. They were found guilty on a string of armed robberies combined with assaults on customers and bank employees. These are the people we hope to find."

"That doesn't bother me. I was in the military police and had to deal with people trained to fight daily."

"Good, I just thought you should know what you're getting yourself into before you sign on. We have a small command center set up just east of Hart. When do you think you can be here?"

"I just need to throw some provisions together." Cache didn't want him to know that she had already packed her backpack. "And we may need to seek some shelter when night falls. I'll make some calls and be there in forty-five minutes."

"Excellent. When you get here I'll introduce you to the team and then we can head out to look for our prisoners."

"Can I ask you how they escaped?" Cache asked.

"We'll go over what we know when you get here. I would ask that you not discuss this with friends or family; we're trying to keep the media out of this for now."

Cache thanked him for the phone call and told him she would meet him shortly. She grabbed her parents' address book and made calls to Ross Henderson, Arthur Shellington and Frank Myers to explain that she was leading a group of law enforcement officers up into the backcountry to look for the escaped prisoners and asked their permission to use their cabins for shelter if the need were to arise. Ross and Arthur agreed without hesitation, while Frank put up a bit of a fuss, though he relented when he appreciated that there might be nothing he could do if they sought shelter at his cabin. Cache collected her firearms and backpack and said goodbye to her parents, promising both that she would exercise caution.

Cache drove from the ranch, which lay west of Hart, along Interstate 90 to arrive at a small command site just east of town. The visibility was poor, and she'd listened to weather updates along the way to gain some sense of what the next twenty-four hours would look like. She pulled her mother's truck in front of a small portable building on wheels with the shield of the Quinn Police Department painted on the side. There were several police cars, SUVs and snowmobiles parked in front of the trailer. Cache made her way into the small structure. The facility housed a small communications center where a female officer wearing a headset was feeding information to other parties. To the left of her was a small meeting area where four men huddled around a white tabletop with gray rusted steel braces holding it up. There were several maps laid out across the table and they seemed to be discussing the locations to search. Along the walls were maps of the surrounding area, police photographs of the fugitives and several other photographs Cache couldn't really make out from her viewpoint. As the men were talking, a tall, slender man with sandy brown hair looked up.

"Miss, this is a police command center, you're not allowed to be here; we ask press to wait outside until we are prepared to make an update."

"I think this is where I'm supposed to be. I'm your guide. My name is Cache Iron."

The man in the middle, with gray hair, mustache and beard, smiled. "I see you found the place. Come on in; you can set your pack down over there, along with your rifle." He walked over and extended his hand. "We talked earlier. I'm Sergeant Malone." Cache shook his hand as he grabbed her by the elbow and brought her over to the group. He introduced the man who had spoken to Cache first as Lieutenant Bryan Stellps, who was in charge of the operation, the officer to the lieutenant's right as Officer Doug Ketchins and the officer to the left as Officer Sam Wallace. Cache assessed that Officer Ketchins was about thirty-eight years of age and Officer Wallace was around forty years old, a little heavier in the gut, balding, with just a bit of hair off to the side.

"We're just going over the details of where we plan on starting." Sergeant Malone pointed to a place north of town and asked Cache her thoughts.

"The area is predominantly flat and there are few rocks until we get to this position." She pointed to a spot on the map. "We can use snowmobiles to reach this spot, but given the lay of the land and the fierceness of the storm, we'd do better to go on foot from this place forward. How many teams are there?"

"Well, you're looking at it. It will be you, Angelo"—he pointed to Sergeant Malone—"Sam, Doug, and of course Hogan, and one more if he ever gets his butt here."

Cache looked around the room and noticed a German shepherd off in the corner, lying on the floor. "I take it that's Hogan?" she said.

"That's Hogan. We've been together for the past decade. I think he'll be able to help us track the guys we're looking for," Sam said.

With that the door opened and a huge of gust of snow followed the man who entered. He stood at approximately six feet tall as he pulled off his balaclava, and had dark brown hair with a neatly trimmed beard. He held the door open for the communications officer as she headed for the exit. He leaned over and whispered something into her ear. She put her hand against his chest, giggled and exited the building.

"About time you got here. Goddamn detectives think they can keep banker's hours," the lieutenant said.

"Sorry I'm late, we think one of my boys is coming down

with something." He looked around the room and noticed someone new. He walked up to Cache, smiled and said, "Who's the badge bunny?" and patted her ass with his hand. Cache's instincts kicked in, and she grabbed him by the wrist and twisted it upward, bringing him to his knees.

"Sorry, my bad, ouch, ouch, please, can you stop that?" the detective said.

"Ms. Iron, we kind of need him, so please don't break him until we get the task done, then you have my permission to beat the crap out of him," the lieutenant said.

She released his wrist and let him get to his feet with whatever dignity he still had.

"Cache, I would like to introduce you to Detective Regan. He was one of the lead detectives involved in the original capture of the Bolden brothers. Detective Regan Fox, I would like you to meet Cache Iron, who is responsible for ensuring you survive your trip out into the wilderness and don't come back here looking like an ice cube."

Cache extended her hand to Regan. Up close she could tell he was six feet two inches and had an athletic build and crystal-blue eyes. He smelled like a mix of musk and wildflowers. As far as men went, he was beautiful. He unzipped his jacket to reveal a white pressed shirt and tweed vest underneath. Combined with a pair of designer jeans, he might have been a model rather than a police officer. The overhead fluorescent lights caused the gold Rolex on his right wrist to sparkle. As she eyed him up and down, she realized that in normal circumstances he would be the type she would go after, setting aside the facial hair. Maybe I should put that hand back, she thought. He pulled off his black leather gloves and put them down on the table. Then she noticed the wedding ring on his finger. He shook her hand and apologized for the ass grabbing, as he'd figured she was just another police groupie who somehow had made her way into the command center.

"Regan, this is where we'll start from. You can take the snowmobiles in to this point and will go on foot per Cache's recommendation from there," the lieutenant said.

"Lieutenant, you said it's only us; why are there not more people going out?" Cache asked.

"As you can see outside, the weather has caused some issues for us. Accidents up and down the highway are pulling police resources elsewhere, and the weather won't support any aircraft. The only team we could assemble was the five of you plus Hogan. As resources become available, we'll deploy more officers to the field, but the longer we hold off, the farther these prisoners can get, and we don't want to put people in harm's way."

"So, Regan, you've spoken to the officers who investigated the prison break. What can you tell us?" the Lieutenant asked.

"Not much. The prisoners were being transported from the prison in Quinn to the state penitentiary in Deer Lodge."

"Do we know why now? Why do a transfer in this weather?" Sam asked.

"Near as we can tell—no one is officially saying this—the warden at Quinn has been taking some heat regarding the Bolden brothers. About a month ago, they almost broke out, hiding in the back of a sewage truck. Luckily, they were discovered before they could make their getaway," Regan said.

"*Sewage* is the right word for those two pieces of crap," Doug said.

"Doug, we talked about this," the lieutenant said.

The men looked at each other, but none would share with Cache what they had discussed prior to her arrival.

Regan continued to fill in everybody on what they believed had happened along the route between prisons. "According to logs, as the prison transport was coming along the highway, they encountered a female motorist whose car had broken down. Standard procedure required them to call it in but continue on their route without stopping. Normally local law enforcement would be dispatched to provide assistance. The recorded conversation suggested that she was not properly dressed for the weather and the officers feared she might not survive, given the storm they were driving in, so they pulled over."

"And we think the female motorist helped the Boldens to escape, or do we think they somehow got the advantage and took her as a hostage?" the lieutenant asked.

"We believe she helped in the escape. We found Corrections Officer Jackson, who drove the prison transport bus, shot at close range from the bus's front door. Corrections Officer Garcia was also found shot at close range, and we found his body lying on the ground just outside of the prison bus. The vehicle in question was discovered about forty miles west of where the bus stopped, which is where we are now."

"Did they radio in a description of the woman?" the lieutenant asked.

"Negative, we have no idea what she looks like," Regan said.

"Sam, what did your guys find out about the abandoned vehicle?" the lieutenant asked.

"We have gone through the vehicle; it was reported stolen a few days ago in Wyoming. The only fingerprints that we've been able to process were from Terry and Leo

Bolden, nothing on the steering wheel; it looks like it was wiped down. We found prison jumpsuits in the trunk, a pair of bolt cutters and the partial remains of footprints in the snow around the vehicle heading in a northern direction," Sam said.

"Why did they abandon the vehicle? Did something happen?" Cache asked.

"The road surfaces were slick and the vehicle they stole didn't have winter tires or chains, so it appears they hit a slick surface and skidded off into a ditch. If they waited for someone to come along, given the number of officers traveling up and down the highway, they risked being caught, so it appears they fled on foot," Doug said.

"So nothing to go on from the car?" the lieutenant asked.

"The only thing to note was a few strands of long red hair on the headrest of the driver's seat."

"Well, that is something."

"Well, maybe not. The owner of the vehicle in Wyoming has red hair, so we don't know if it's hers or it belongs to the person we're looking for."

"Have you run it through the system for a DNA check?"

"We found no hair follicles on the strands to do a DNA check on."

"Regan, that girlfriend of Terry's—what was her name?" the lieutenant asked.

Regan reached for his notebook and flipped through the pages. "Let's see, I believe it was Hannah O'Conner."

"She a redhead?"

"Blond from what I can remember, but she could have dyed it."

The lieutenant held his hand to his mouth, and he muttered a few things Cache couldn't make out.

"Okay, so you guys and gals formulate your plan and

head out, and be careful out there; no telling what you're in for. Doug, a moment before you go."

Doug and the lieutenant walked over to the communications area. They continued to discuss something that was not audible from where Cache stood; however, she noticed that the lieutenant handed something to Doug that he seemed to tuck inside his jacket. He then returned to the group, who made their way outside. The department had brought up five snowmobiles and a carrier for Hogan, and the group fired them up and headed north toward Saugeen Mountain. The snow was thick in some places, attributable to an increase in moisture in the snow, as the snowmobiles raced along the path that Cache had outlined. It would take them about an hour to get to the place where they would need to leave the snowmobiles behind and continue their search on foot. As the group moved across the white-covered fields, they would take breaks every ten to fifteen minutes to survey the surrounding area with binoculars. Ranchers had made earlier sightings of three individuals in dark clothing making their way north. The snow was coming down so heavily it felt like they were trying to look at something with a white sheet over their eyes. Cache could spot very little sign of any movement from animal or human.

After fifty minutes they came to a spot where the rocks were more abundant as they found themselves near the base of Saugeen Mountain. They pulled the snowmobiles in tight and disconnected the batteries to ensure that no one came along and used the machines to aid in their escape. The five of them gathered around Cache's snowmobile, where she placed down a paper map and a compass. Angelo pointed to the map and Cache pointed out their route. To cover more ground, the group would split off into two smaller groups and move out at a forty-five-degree angle to each other for about sixty minutes, then move in the opposite directions, creating a diamond shape. Eventually both parties should meet at a point that Cache had identified on the map. It would get dark in the next four hours, and then the group would need to seek shelter for the evening. Based on the area Angelo wanted to cover, Cache suggested that they plan to shelter from the storm overnight at Ross Henderson's cabin.

"Where on the map is his cabin?" Angelo asked.

"He's right here, which will be about thirty minutes from the point where both parties should intersect in your diamond search pattern."

"Are there any other cabins up here?" he asked.

"There are three cabins that I know about. All the men are friends of the family and have given permission for us to use them. The Henderson cabin is here"—Cache pointed to the location on the map—"the Shellington cabin is here"—Cache pointed to a location west of the diamond search pattern—"and the Myers cabin is located here," she said as she pointed to a location west of the Shellington cabin.

"Okay, so Cache and I will go in this direction, Doug, you, Regan, Sam and Hogan go in this direction. I don't know if we'll have continuous communication while we're out here, but if anyone gets into trouble, fire a shot in the air."

The two groups moved away from each other, heading in opposite directions. As Cache walked with Angelo, the snow they were traversing was thick and each step brought it up to their knees. There were trees all around them, and in certain areas they provided protection from the fierce winds. Shoots of long grass rose from the snow in random patches. All the party were well attired for the storm, including

Hogan, who had small boots to protect his paws. As Cache and Angelo walked along the chosen path, they stopped every five minutes to search the horizon for any sign of movement or tracks.

"Can I ask you something?" Cache asked.

"Sure, what's on your mind?"

"Was it wise that we split up like this? It's not like you have two guides."

"Unfortunately, we have to cover as much ground as possible. I'm counting on Hogan to help guide them. Besides, I felt that if you and Regan were together, only you would come back alive."

"Regan is all talk, no bite. I've dealt with his kind most of my life."

"How do you handle it?"

"Like I did at the command center: I put them on their knees begging for mercy."

Angelo laughed, though his balaclava hid any hint of a smile.

After they'd walked through the snow for about an hour, Cache motioned to Angelo that they should start to make their way in the opposite direction so they could meet the other group at the designated point. Angelo grabbed his walkie-talkie to signal to the other group that they were making the planned change to their route and the others should think about doing the same.

Static came from the speaker as Angelo turned up the volume on his walkie-talkie.

"Doug, you there? Can you hear me?"

No response came from the other party.

"Regan, Sam, can you hear me? If anyone can hear me, please pick up."

Static was the only sound coming from his communications device.

"If anyone can hear me, we are adjusting our path and should meet you at the rendezvous point in one hour."

Still no response came.

As they moved along the adjusted path, the snow grew deeper and deeper, slowing down each step and draining their energy as they moved along. After about fifteen minutes, Angelo thought he heard Doug's voice come from his walkie-talkie. He grabbed it off of his belt and pressed the button to speak.

"Doug, is that you?" Angelo asked.

"What the hell are you doing?" came from the walkie-talkie.

With that, there was nothing but silence, until the sound of thunder echoed through the area. One rumble, a second, a third, a fourth and then silence.

Angelo looked at Cache. "That wasn't thunder, was it?"

"No, worse, that sounded like gunfire."

Cache and Angelo ran as fast as they could through the deep snow, heading in the direction they believed the gunfire had originated from. The deepening snow made it feel like each one was pulling a heavy weighted wagon behind them, until they reached an area surrounded by pine trees from which the shots had come.

3

TWO KILLED WITH ONE STONE

A s Cache and Angelo made their way into the clearing surrounded by pine trees in all directions, the snow slowed up. The trees were acting as a wall to hold the storm back. On the ground in front of them was the body of someone lying on their back as red blood stained the snow, like a dropped glass of red wine on a white carpet. Cache pulled her rifle from her back and gripped the stock with her finger on the trigger. Angelo reached for his handgun and cupped the grip with both hands as they crept slowly toward the body.

The individual lay sprawled out in a spread-eagle position, wearing jeans and a dark blue jacket with a face mask. His legs were in the seven and five positions, his hands at ten and two. A small black pistol was sticking out of the snow approximately three feet from the victim's left hand. Cache and Angelo kneeled by the body, and Angelo put his fingers on the victim's neck to feel for a pulse. He looked at Cache and shook his head. Angelo grabbed the bottom of the face mask and pulled it off the victim's head. A long, narrow face; chiseled features; and surfer-blond hair. The victim was unmistakably Terry Bolden. Cache could see three bullet holes in a tight pattern on his chest, with the dark stain of blood on the fabric.

"Well, that's one less person we have to find," Angelo said.

They both looked around the area until Angelo caught sight of what appeared to be another body about forty feet away.

He tapped Cache on the shoulder and pointed to what he saw. Cache gripped her rifle tighter and stood up as Angelo motioned for her to stay put. He moved along the ground while crouched down, holding his handgun with both hands. Cache steadied herself in the snow and raised her rifle to brace the stock against her shoulder. Angelo reached the body of the second individual and stopped and looked down. He observed the word *Police* stitched on the second victim's shoulders as he pulled the blue balaclava from the man's face. Dead in the snow with a single bullet to the front of the head was Officer Doug Ketchins. Angelo checked for a pulse, but the officer was gone. Cache saw Angelo with his head in his hand and knew something was up. She got to her feet, lowered her rifle and walked over. Staring down, she could see the face of Doug Ketchins looking up at her. Angelo reached down and closed the eyelids of the officer.

"What do you think happened here?" Cache asked.

Angelo pulled his balaclava off and rubbed his chin with his hand. He looked back at the body of Terry Bolden and then looked at the body of Doug Ketchins. He kept rubbing his face, muttering to himself.

Cache looked at both men, dead in the snow.

"You know this makes little sense," Cache said.

Angelo stood up and looked at her. "I know, it doesn't add up."

"There are two scenarios; neither makes any sense."

"Scenario one: Doug catches Terry Bolden and shoots him three times in the chest, and as Terry falls to the ground, he gets a lucky shot off, hitting Doug straight in the head," Angelo said.

Cache jumped in. "And then scenario two: Terry catches Doug and shoots him in the head, and he manages three shots to the chest, or someone else shoots Terry, but who? If it was Regan or Sam, wouldn't they be here?" Cache asked.

"Unless they're off in the snow somewhere hurt. We should check around. You go over there, I'll check over here and we'll meet back in the middle." As the two circled the area, there was no sign of Regan or Sam anywhere. Cache observed a set of tracks that led from the edge of the clearing to the middle, where both men were located. As she continued searching around the area, she ran into Angelo coming from the other direction.

"Do you notice any sign of them?" Angelo asked.

"Not of them, but I found a set of footprints leading to the midpoint near the two bodies, and judging by the size of the indentations in the snow, my guess is it was a male that made them," Cache said.

"That's interesting, but if it was Regan or Sam, where are they now?"

"Maybe they happened onto it and have given chase."

Angelo picked up the walkie-talkie and pressed down the button to speak.

"Sam, Regan, are you there?" A few seconds of silence passed before a voice came over the walkie-talkie.

"Sam here, Angelo, are you okay?"

"Yeah, Cache and I are okay, where are you and Regan at?" Angelo asked.

"I don't know about Regan. Hogan and I are here, somewhere. Did you hear those shots?"

"Yeah, we found the source."

"What was it?"

"Will talk when you get here."

"How am I supposed to do that? You have the guide."

Angelo looked over to Cache. "Any ideas?"

"Always."

Cache kneeled down and took off her backpack. She pulled a flare gun from her pack and loaded it up.

"Were you a Boy Scout?" Angelo asked, looking at her.

"Nah, just an Iron."

Angelo advised Sam to watch for a flare in the sky as Cache stood up and shot the flare up overhead. Angelo and Cache returned to the clearing to examine the bodies. Cache went to investigate Terry and left Angelo to deal with Doug. Cache looked at the lifeless body of Terry Bolden, his crystal-blue eyes staring back at her. She closed his eyelids and opened up his jacket. Cache searched the pockets and found most were empty, except for an inside pocket that held a small piece of folded-up paper. She opened up the paper to see that the top edge had been torn away from something and read three names written in pencil: Grover Brown, Horace Miller, and Rufus Williams. She folded the paper back up and tucked it into her inside pocket. His remaining pockets were empty. She caught sight of a few long strands of red hair on his white shirt beneath his jacket.

She glanced back at Angelo and wanted to share the list with him, but he seemed occupied as he talked to the corpse of his friend.

"Oh my god."

Cache looked in the voice's direction as Sam and Hogan made their way into the area. Sam ran to the body of Doug Ketchins and kneeled down beside him. Hogan walked over to his face, licked the side of his cheek and lay down in the snow. Cache stood up and walked over to join the men surrounding Doug's body.

"What happened?" Sam asked, looking up at Angelo.

"At this point your guess is as good as mine. We found him that way," Cache said.

Sam glanced over at Cache. "That's not Regan, is it?"

"No, that is the lovely Terry Bolden, former resident of Quinn prison."

"And you shot him?" Sam asked.

"Nope, we found both men dead, thought maybe you or Regan might have killed Terry after he killed Doug."

"Wasn't me. About thirty minutes after we left the two of you, we spotted what looked like a man running through the woods. I turned to Doug and Regan to formulate a plan for capture and the two of them had disappeared. I then radioed you but got nothing but static. Hogan and I gave pursuit, but the deep snow slowed us down, and by the time we got to where we'd spotted the individual, they were gone and Doug and Regan were nowhere to be seen.

"You know, he wasn't supposed to be out here," Sam said.

"Who, Doug?" Cache asked.

Before Sam could respond, Angelo interrupted the conversation. "I told the lieutenant that, and it's not something we should discuss outside of the department. Sorry, Cache, no offense."

As the three of them stood over Doug's body talking about the events and hypothesizing about how they may have occurred, Hogan's ears popped up as Regan made his way into the clearing.

"Thank you to whoever sent up that flare, I thought I would be lost forever."

"Well, not forever, but at least until spring," Cache said.

Regan kneeled down and looked at the body, then up at Angelo. "What happened?"

"We're trying to figure that out, and since you're the detective, why don't you detect? What have you got there?" Angelo asked, noticing that Regan appeared to be holding a new red backpack.

Regan dropped it by his feet. "Got separated from the others, spotted someone and chased after them. Lost sight of them with the poor visibility when I came across this backpack in the snow. The identification inside shows it belongs to a Kyle Fleming."

"So, some hiker lost his backpack, may have been there for months," Sam said.

"It looks intact; animals would have torn through it looking for food if they found it, so it's probably been out here only a short time," Cache said.

Angelo's expression showed anything but happiness.

"Kyle Fleming, what is he doing up here in this weather?" Angelo said.

"My guess is the same as us, except I don't think he's planning on capturing anybody," Regan said.

"So, can I ask who Kyle Fleming is?" Cache asked.

"Kyle is someone connected with the Bolden brothers, and not in a good way."

"Could he have done this?"

"Oh yeah, he could have done this," Regan said.

Regan looked at the group, first at Sam, then Angelo and Cache, and noticed something in the snow behind Cache.

"That's not another body?"

"Yeah, that's Terry Bolden. Three shots to the chest, was dead when we found him."

Regan parted from the group and walked over to where Terry's body lay. His back to the rest of the group, Regan eyed the corpse up and down and noticed that his jacket was open. He turned to face the group. "Hey, did you guys search the body?"

Cache spoke up. "Yeah, I had a look, didn't find much."

"When you say *much*, what does that mean?"

"A few strands of long red hair are still on his white T-shirt if you look closely."

"Anything else?"

Cache thought about the piece of paper she had found. She had yet to share the details with Angelo and for now kept it to herself. "Nope, nothing, just the red hair." Cache turned to Angelo and whispered in his ear, "I found something, but I wanted to share it with you first."

"Good idea, keep it to yourself until we can talk in private."

Regan crouched down over Terry's body and went through his pockets.

"Thinking I missed something?" Cache asked.

"Just doing my job. Always a good idea to have a second set of eyes looking at everything, that's what my old partner used to tell me."

Regan finished searching the body and returned to the group huddled around the body of Doug Ketchins.

Angelo looked around at the sky. The snow was still falling, but what light had existed was disappearing for the day. He looked at Cache. "What do you think, should we head to that cabin you talked about?"

"Yeah, we should get a move on. The trees are blocking

the snow, but as soon as we leave the clearing, we're back to poor visibility. I'm guessing we have about forty minutes of actual daylight and then we'll be trying to make it there in the dark."

"What are we going to do with the bodies? We can't just leave them here," Regan said.

"That is precisely what we will do with them. The snow is deep getting here, and I don't fancy trying to navigate in the darkness with a dead body over my shoulder. We'll take all of Doug's personal effects and photograph the bodies with our smartphones, then we need to head out, unless you want to carry them," Angelo said.

Regan looked at both bodies and thought for a few minutes. Trying to rig up something to transport the bodies on would take too much time and would consume what daylight they had left. Then there was the question of whether the bodies would come inside or stay outside of the cabin. He knew that the animals would sniff out the remains and the corpses might be missing by morning. He looked back at the dead body of Terry Bolden and thought that might just work fine. As he turned back to the group, he could see Angelo photographing Doug's body and then removing his personal effects. He then noticed that Angelo seemed frustrated as he was playing around with the inside of Doug's coat.

"Need a hand?" he asked.

"I'm okay, I just got to get this device that Doug was wearing."

The group watched as Angelo freed a small black device the size of a cigarette pack from the inside of Doug's jacket.

"What have you got there, Angelo?" Sam asked.

"Given Doug's history with the fugitives, the lieutenant made him wear this device. You see this small badge on his jacket?" Angelo pointed to a small badge with a black dot in the middle. "It's actually a camera; it's been recording the whole time we've been out here. When we get back to the station, we can upload it to a computer and see what happened here."

"Well, that's clever. Didn't think to share with us?" Sam asked.

"You know, Angelo, I should hold on to that for safe-keeping," Regan said, stretching out his hand.

"If it's all the same to you, I will hold on to it for now," Angelo said, and took the small black device and put it down deep into his backpack. Cache noted a sense of frustration on Regan's face. The expression you might get when someone is talking down to you.

Cache took out her map from her backpack, consulted her compass and checked with her smartphone to see if she could determine their position. Fortunately, despite the poor cellular signal from the storm, the GPS, while spotty, still gave her a sense of where they were. She motioned for the group to follow her and they made their way out of the tree line into freezing winds and lashing snow. As they hiked toward the cabin, she could hear the men behind her bickering. Regan could not seem to let go of the fact that Angelo had taken possession of the recording device and kept trying to convince Angelo that it needed to be with him. She thought about the three names on the piece of paper she had taken from Terry's body and reflected on whether it was wise to not share with the group. After all, she was no longer a policewoman; her role was to act as a guide. Though something kept nagging her about the three names on the list. Grover and Horace; she couldn't think of anyone she had ever met with either of those names, and they were not common. No mother looked down at her newborn and said, "You look like a Grover."

The snow continued to deepen as they pushed forward. With each step they became more strained, breathing deeper as the chilled air filled their lungs and froze the hairs on the inside of their noses until the nostrils closed as if the sides were stuck together. With each passing step, her feet would sink down into the snow until it came up to the middle of her thigh. The snow had become too deep for Hogan to manage and Sam had opted to carry him, sharing the duty with Angelo as they trudged along in the storm.

Where are the other two people we're looking for? she thought. Unless they seek shelter from the storm, they may very well be dead by the time we find them. Who is Kyle Fleming, and could he be helping the Boldens to escape? She looked back at them as they huffed and puffed, their breath freezing in the air in front of their faces. Men could be so aggravating sometimes. She kept going over the facts that had presented themselves to her, so intent on her thoughts that she failed to appreciate that they were not alone. As they pushed forward, her ears finally picked up something that had probably been there for some time. She raised her hand to indicate for the group behind her to stop as she put her hand on the Beretta M9 strapped to her belt.

She could hear a howl close by, and then another. Hogan barked in response as Cache threw back a glance at Sam that lost its effect with her face covering. She put her finger over her mouth to show that they should be quiet, but before Sam could put his hand around Hogan's snout, he let out a series of barks that would solidify their position to those watching them. The howls grew louder and then there was just silence. The snow fell all around them; they had visibility for about ten feet as Cache surveyed the area in all directions. Cache drew out her weapon, and Regan and Angelo followed suit as Sam clutched Hogan in his arms. The three of them circled around Sam and Hogan, weapons drawn, and yet there was no sound. Cache felt the adrenaline rush through her veins, and she knew instinctively to take deep breaths and center herself.

She didn't see where the attack came from; she looked behind her as a group of wolves descended on their position, the lead wolf jumping onto Angelo and seizing his arm with his teeth. Angelo screamed for them to get the wolf off of him. Sam dropped Hogan to reach for his pistol as Hogan attacked one wolf in the pack. Cache counted five in total as the wolves moved in all directions, their white and gray coats blending with the environment. Regan seemed to shoot in the air, while Sam tried to kick the wolf attacking Angelo to persuade him to leave, as a shot may as easily have hit Angelo as the wolf.

Cache fixated on one wolf and squeezed her trigger, dropping the animal in the snow. Hogan seemed to be in a fight with the wolf farthest from the pack, and Cache could see the jaws of the wolf come in contact with Hogan's neck. She feared she might not be able to protect him. Hogan responded, fangs showing, as the wolf bloodline emerged from the German shepherd. Cache turned her attention to Sam, who was trying to free Angelo from the jaws of the pack's leader. A noise of a wounded animal echoed behind her. Cache turned back to see where Hogan was, but he wasn't visible to her. She then spotted a wolf in the ten o'clock position from her and fired two more rounds, bringing the beast to its knees. Sam continued to try to pull the wolf off Angelo. Regan fired toward one of the two remaining attackers, causing it to retreat into the night. Cache holstered her handgun and took her rifle from her shoulder. She pushed Sam out of the way, grabbed the barrel of the rifle with two hands and swung it like a bat, hitting the wolf near its head. The wolf flew back into the snow as Cache grabbed for the stock of her rifle, and then three shots and the leader of the pack was gone. Regan finally hit something, unloading his gun into the wolf.

Sam ran to Hogan's last position as Cache kneeled down beside Angelo to examine the bite marks to his arm. As she pulled the heavy parka up away from his skin, she smiled. The thick jacket had taken most of the beating. There was no sign of injury to his arm. She looked behind her to Sam's position and could see him petting Hogan's head.

"His paw is hurt, but he is alive," he yelled.

Cache looked at Angelo and asked if he was okay enough to stand. When he made it to his feet, Cache moved over to where Hogan was, his tail wagging. There were bite marks to his front right paw and traces of blood around his mouth. The trail of blood that stained the snow heading away from the group was evidence that it was not his blood on his face. Sam asked her if she could look for a first-aid kit he kept for Hogan in the pack on his back, and Cache opened up the flap and rummaged inside of it. She found clothes, cartridges, food and handcuffs, and came across a small photo of a woman tucked into the side of his pack. Cache flipped it over and read, *Can't wait until we can be together —Nancy*. She put it back and found the kit right at the bottom of the bag. "You had to put it at the bottom, didn't you?"

She handed the kit to Sam, who worked to look after Hogan's wound. Cache stood up and studied the area. She focused on the route they would need to continue on and grabbed a flashlight from her backpack that she could attach to her belt. The daylight had disappeared, and they were now in the darkness as snow continued to fall.

"I think Hogan is out of commission. We'll need to take turns carrying him." Sam said.

"How far to the cabin, do you reckon?" Angelo asked.

"I'm guessing we have another twenty minutes if we're lucky. If everyone is okay, we better get a move on."

They continued along their route until a small wooden structure became visible to them and they made a direct path there as fast as their weary legs would take them. As they approached the cabin, Cache raised her hand for the group to stop.

"What's wrong?" Angelo asked.

"I'm looking for signs of movement. We're not the only ones out here looking for shelter. I'm just wondering if something is sitting in the darkness, waiting for us to open the door."

4

PORT IN THE STORM

Cache and Sam put their shoulders against the door and pushed it open to reveal a small cabin with a stone fireplace, a set of bunk beds, a cramped kitchen and chairs positioned around the fireplace. A meager window near the west side of the structure was closed tight with wooden shutters, and a large wooden beam running across the inside prevented the window from being opened from the outside. The four individuals walked into the darkness of the cabin as Cache pulled the flashlight from her belt and shone it around the room to see what they were dealing with. Angelo looked around the room as Regan closed the wooden door behind him and latched it shut from the inside.

Something scurried along the floor as they looked around for a source of light. Two half-rusted green kerosene lanterns sat on the small table in front of the fireplace. Cache picked up the first and shook it to determine if there was kerosene sloshing around inside. She then did the same for the second and grinned at the sound that she heard. Cache didn't know how much fuel was in each, but she figured it should be enough until they could get a fire going. She grabbed her flip lighter with interlocking flintlocks engraved on the side and lit the wicks of both lanterns, which yielded a warm glow that helped banish some darkness. Sheltered from the outside, they could hear the winds whistling as they found their way down the chimney. The cabin floorboards were uneven and rotting in some spots; they creaked as they made their way over them.

"It's not much, but at least we're not out there."

"Man, it feels like a meat freezer in here," said Regan.

As they exhaled, the expelled air looked like white smoke in front of their faces.

Regan looked at Cache. "You know, Cache, I could think of a way the two of us might stay warm together."

Before Cache could respond, Sam spoke up. "Shut the fuck up, Regan, I don't appreciate it and I'm sure she doesn't either."

"Hey, just trying to lighten the mood," replied Regan.

Cache wandered over to the fireplace and picked up an ax that lay against the wall.

"Cache, I was only kidding, just cop humor. You were a cop once, you understand these things," said Regan.

"Please, if I wanted to kill you, I would have shot you dead hours ago," she said. "We need wood to get a fire going or we could still die of hypothermia tonight, and I would rather die on my own than huddle up with you, Regan. I think I would rather take my chances with a grizzly."

Angelo reached for the ax, but Cache pulled away. "What are you doing? It's mine."

"If anyone should go out in this storm and chop wood, it should be one of us."

Cache's eyes narrowed, and her lips crinkled. "Why, because I'm a woman? I'm not pregnant, and even if I was, I can still bring down a tree faster than the three of you combined. You're more likely to come back having cut a toe off. No, I'll get the wood. Mr. Henderson said there might be some provisions in the cabin and a little whiskey, so why don't you gentlemen try to determine what we have to consume and I'll be back." Cache walked over to Hogan and petted his head. "You're in charge, Hogan, until I get back." With that, Cache opened the door and walked outside into the raging storm.

After forty minutes had passed as the officers sat in the chairs surrounding the fireplace, they were starting to worry that maybe something had happened to Cache and that she wasn't as tough as she made herself out to be.

"You realize we stand a better chance of survival with her if this storm doesn't let up. Perhaps we should go look for her," Regan said.

The door flew open as Cache carried in a bunch of chopped logs.

"I stacked some additional logs outside, in case we run low in the middle of the night." She dropped what she was carrying in front of the fireplace and grabbed her lighter from her pocket and some fuel from her backpack. She formed a pyramid with the wood in the fireplace and after several minutes had gotten a fire started that edged out the icy air in the cabin with warmth. The three men had foraged around the cabin in Cache's absence to locate what food the owner had stored away, along with a few open bottles of whiskey. The group sat around the fire, pulling food from their backpacks and sharing with each other as they got to know each other better. Cache seemed to be the best prepared, the result of military training and an overprotective father.

"Hey, Angelo, I heard you pulled the pin. How many years has it been?" Sam asked.

"Too many; it will be thirty years next month," said Angelo.

"Any plans?"

"Heading to California, tired of these winters," said Angelo.

"You married?" Cache asked.

"Was. Problems with this job, late hours, being called out at any time and the sheer worry that I might not come home some night led to our divorce. Now it's just me."

"What are your plans in California?" Regan asked.

"Don't know, I might open up a bar or something, just don't want to be a cop anymore."

"Well, hopefully we'll get these guys, or the weather will, and you can ride off into the sunset," Sam said.

"I just wish Doug hadn't."

"I know, so do all of us. At least he got the bastard for what he did to his wife. If I had caught Terry, I might have done the same."

"No, you wouldn't, you would have arrested him, because that is what we do. Doug shouldn't have been here in the first place; too close to the case. Others were out sick or dealing with accidents along the highway and we needed to get boots on the ground if we were going to stand a chance at catching these two."

"What about you, Regan? I noticed that gold ring on your finger you keep playing with," Cache said.

"Yeah, a few years now, met Liz some years after I lost the love of my life."

"That's rough. Did she die?"

"No, not that dramatic, we just had obstacles that we couldn't overcome. But then I met Liz, the second love of my life." Regan reached into a pocket, pulled out his wallet and flipped to a picture of him, his wife and their two boys and handed it to Cache.

"Nice family. Two boys, that must be a handful. What are their names?"

"The eldest is Tim, and the youngest is David; their mother does most of the discipline. I just want them to have a better childhood than I had."

"Rough childhood?" Sam asked.

"No harder than some. Money was tight, we didn't have much; that's why I want my boys to have everything."

Cache flipped the photograph over to see a wedding picture of what looked like a younger Regan and his wife, Liz. She noticed that he was clean shaven in the snapshot with a cleft in his chin. Cache thought about how much she liked a guy with a cleft in his chin; there was something rugged about the look. She flipped to the only other photograph in his wallet, a black-and-white picture of a family: a young boy, two girls and a set of parents. What must it be like to grow up with older sisters?

Cache looked at the three of them as they sat around in a circle in front of the fireplace. The logs crackled. The door creaked, and the winds outside screamed as they hit the small cabin.

"What happened to Doug's wife, if I can ask," Cache said, sensing this was a sensitive topic. Her role was to act as a guide on this trip, so they may not have wanted to share details in too much depth with her.

"How much do you know about the Bolden brothers?" Angelo asked.

"Not much. When you hired me, I did a quick search on the internet, found out they were bank robbers suspected of multiple murders with no evidence and something about a relationship with one or more of the bank employees," Cache said.

"That's pretty much it. They robbed five banks until Regan and his partner got a call one day that they had been spotted going into the fifth bank."

Cache looked at Regan, who said, "Yeah, we got a lucky break that day. Someone recognized the two and called it in. By the time they walked out of the bank, we had the place surrounded. I always figured they would go down in a hail of bullets like Bonnie and Clyde, but they surrendered," Regan said.

"And they dated the employees of the banks they robbed? What are the chances that's a coincidence?"

"Zero," Regan said. "We figured out that they would scout out the branches of various banks and would then search on different websites for female bank employees looking for a relationship. They then dated the women to learn everything they could about the bank."

"That must have taken some time, to browse through thousands of profiles, hoping to strike pay dirt," Cache said.

"Not these two; they got help. As near as we figured, they had an accomplice. The boys would go into a bank with those small spy cameras you can buy online and capture images of everyone in the bank. Then they had an accomplice who was brilliant enough to hack various local websites, comparing the scanned images with images on the sites to determine which females were out there looking for someone to connect with."

"Regan, do you think it was Terry's girlfriend that might have done the hacking?" Angelo asked.

"Nah, she was a sweet girl, mixed up with the wrong guy. My partner investigated her and said she didn't have the skills to pull it off, but she had the looks."

"What do you mean by that?" Cache asked.

"Smoking hot," Regan said. "All she had to do was find a hacker somewhere with the skills to pull it off and drop those pants, and one look at her hot-pink thong with black frilly lace and those computer nerds would do whatever she asked."

"'Hot-pink thong'? That's a pretty detailed description, Regan, where did you come up with that?" Sam asked.

"I don't know, just popped in my head. Cache, help me out here, that's common for girls these days?"

"We are not talking about my underwear."

"Probably some stripper he can't get out of his head. I remember what it was like to go out with the boys to blow off steam after a shift. Do I have it right?" Angelo asked.

Regan looked a little flushed by the line of questioning. "Happily married, guys, and if you must know, that is what my wife likes. Anyway, getting back to the story . . .

"So, these guys go out and set up a fake security company online, fake phone number, fake names for each of them under their photos. Plus they grabbed other people's photos they found online to make the company appear large with lots of employees. They then start chatting with the bank employees online through different websites that they belong to. They tell them they work in security, romance them, the whole thing. And the women fall for this. Soon they're dating for real and asking many questions about where they work, the security. And the women, because it's pillow talk, divulge everything."

"Talk about having an inside person," Sam said.

"Yeah, they used their sweethearts to help them plan their heists. Then the day of the robbery, their love interest doesn't show up for work. No one has seen them since," Regan said.

"Their attorney suggested the women were in on it and fled so as not to go to jail. The district attorney had no interest in prosecuting them for the potential killing of the women with what little evidence they had to go on and no bodies. The jury found them guilty on only the bank robberies, along with assaults that took place during the robberies," Angelo said.

"Five robberies. I take it there are five bodies out there somewhere?" Cache asked.

"Someday, a rancher will stumble onto something, and with a DNA match, the victims will get justice," Angelo said.

"Well, Terry already got what was coming to him, but we'll charge Leo," Sam said, "provided we find him."

"That is, if Kyle Fleming doesn't find them first, right, Angelo?" Cache said.

"If Kyle Fleming is up here, you can bet his brother Norman is with him. Best thing that could happen is the Flemings find him and take him out like Terry," Regan said.

"So, what's their deal? Why are they out in a storm looking for these two? They're not cops, are they?" Cache asked.

"Nah, they're out here to settle a score," Angelo said.

"Must be some score to go after escaped prisoners in the middle of a snowstorm. When you encounter an animal out in the wilderness who feels trapped, that is when they are the most dangerous. Nothing to lose; the survival instinct kicks in."

"The first three banks they knocked over were in Wyoming, then they got stupid. They crossed state lines and came into Montana. One bank they were casing, Terry recognized a teller behind the desk. A few years older than when he saw her last, but he realized who she was the moment he caught sight of her," Angelo said.

"Who was she?" Cache asked.

Regan chimed in, "Her name was Nancy Milne—at least that was her married name; before that she was Nancy Fleming. Back when she was Nancy Fleming, she was the girlfriend of Terry's younger brother Ethan."

"Wait, I thought Leo was Terry's younger brother," Cache said.

"There are three brothers in the Bolden family. The eldest was Terry, the middle brother is Ethan, and the youngest is Leo. Anyway, Terry took a liking to Nancy, felt she should date him and not his brother. Made things terrible for the two of them, to the point where they had to break up. She eventually would meet Harvey Milne and get married, though from what I understood it sounded as if Ethan was her genuine love," Regan said.

"That's sad," Cache said. "What happened to Ethan?"

"Fell off the map from what I gathered, Regan, did you ever find him?" Angelo asked.

"My partner Bill and I followed a few leads, but they led nowhere."

"Could these crimes involve Ethan at all?" Cache asked.

"Nah, Ethan was a smart guy—some might even say a genius. He wouldn't get involved directly working with Terry."

Cache turned to Angelo. "You were saying?"

"Well, when Terry spotted Nancy, he became fixated on that being their next bank. From interviews we did with Leo, he knew the risks of crossing state lines, but Terry wouldn't listen. Anyway, they go in flashing weapons like on the previous bank jobs, tell everyone to hit the floor, but instead of focusing on the cash, Terry started focusing on Nancy. Eyewitnesses said he stood behind her wearing a ski mask and speaking into her ear. Witnesses watched as he unbuttoned her blouse and reached his hand in underneath. She later told us he had told her he would take her into the vault for some private time. She also knew his voice from somewhere but couldn't place it."

Angelo paused for a moment to clear his throat and take a shot of whiskey from one of the bottles that were making their way around the circle. "Doug's wife, Betsy, was the assistant manager at the bank and said she could see the sheer terror in Nancy's eyes, so she got to her feet and told Terry to back off. Take the money and leave, she demanded. Well, Terry wasn't used to being told what to do, so he left Nancy alone and moved over to Betsy. She took a severe beating in front of witnesses for uttering those words to him. He tore her blouse open, pulled her skirt up and told her he would screw her so everyone could see. She fought back, screaming at him to get off. He bent her over her desk, and he fumbled around under her skirt with his hand. Her resistance must have frustrated him, because the next thing to happen was he was pounding her face into the desk. After several hits that resulted in a broken nose and losing teeth, he let her fall to the floor, where he kicked her in the gut, screaming at her with every kick. According to witnesses, Leo had been yelling at his brother to stop, but Terry either didn't hear him or ignored him. As a result, she lost the baby she was carrying; she was six weeks pregnant, would have been their first."

"Which is why Doug should not have been up here, Angelo. You recognize it and I recognize it," Regan said.

"Wasn't my call, Regan, that's why they made him wear that body camera," Angelo said. "Anyway, Nancy's brothers must have remembered what Betsy did to look after their little sister, and I guess they feel they owe her. I'm sure if they find Leo before us, Leo could head for the afterlife sooner than he planned."

"So, you think the Flemings killed Terry?" Cache asked.

"You know, if we'd just found Terry's body, I would say that I think there's a strong probability to that, but why kill Doug? If you're there as some payback for what Doug's wife did for their family, don't add up."

"Maybe they killed Terry, and Doug came upon them and would have arrested them, and they shot him to avoid going to jail," Sam said.

"Killing a cop is not the way you avoid jail time, Sam," Regan said.

"Do you have a better explanation?" Sam asked.

The room was silent as all parties pondered the idea that perhaps Doug had found himself in the wrong place at the wrong time and the Fleming brothers had no intention of going to jail. The time passed as the four of them chatted and bonded over stories until Angelo suggested they head to bed, as they would need to get out early in the morning to see if Leo Bolden and his guest could be located. Angelo suggested that Cache take the top bunk while he eyed the bottom bunk, citing age. Regan and Sam pulled the remaining chairs together to form a somewhat uncomfortable bed, but at least they were not sleeping on the floor. Hogan got up and moved to position himself below Sam.

———

At five thirty in the morning, the sound of the floorboards squeaking awoke Cache. She listened for the storm outside, but the winds seemed to have quieted in the middle of the night. She turned over to her side to scan the cabin to determine the source of the noise. The team needed their sleep for the morning's search, and they'd opted not to post a guard through the night. She scanned over toward the door; the light from the fire caused the metal bar across the door to shine. The secured bar ensured nothing had come in from outside. She glanced around the room until she noticed a shadowy figure going through one backpack.

"Hey, what are you doing?" she asked. The figure walked toward her until Cache faced Regan.

"Looking for some company?" he asked.

"No, and what are you doing?" She rose, her elbow underneath her.

"Searching for food in my backpack. Why, what are you concerned about?" he asked.

"That is not your backpack, yours is over by the chair you were sleeping in. The yellow one is mine, and the one next to it, which you were going through, is Angelo's."

"That would explain why I couldn't find my candy bar; thanks."

Regan wandered back to his chair, located his backpack and started rummaging through it. When he found his candy bar, he held it up to show Cache. She just smiled and lay down, staring at the ceiling. She knew she would rise in about a half hour to survey the results of the prior night's storm. Growing up on a ranch, sleeping in was not part of the program, and often they would tend to chores before heading off to school. She interlaced her fingers and put them behind her head. She pondered the crime scene. Was there something they were missing? The tracks in the snow suggested at least three parties had been present at the crime scene, possibly more; some of the tracks could have been filled in by the blowing snow before they arrived on the scene. Why had Doug not called in the capture of Terry Bolden? she thought. Did he have plans to exact his revenge? After what he'd lost, would anyone blame him for wanting his pound of flesh? Still, a seasoned police officer with other criminals in the area would have wanted backup or support. Could the brothers have gotten the drop on Doug and shot him dead? Cache played various scenarios in her head to come up with a plausible explanation for how the two men had died.

After about thirty minutes passed, she had a headache thinking about the players in this situation and hopped down from her bunk. The motion must have woken up Angelo, who had been snoring for part of the night.

"Where are you going?" he asked.

"I'll pop my head outside and see what we're dealing with. Do you hear it?" she asked.

"Hear what? I hear nothing."

"Exactly. The winds have died down over the past few hours, I just want to see what we're dealing with."

Cache walked over to the door and raised the metal bar that secured it. Hogan jumped up and wandered over to her. She pulled the door open. A three-foot snowdrift had accumulated at the door frame, but the skies were clear and the sun was beaming down on the fresh snow. Hogan jumped through the snow drift and went off to do the business a dog does in the morning. The sun on the snow was as a bright as a set of oncoming headlights from a fast-approaching vehicle. Luckily for her she had her shades in her backpack. She went back inside and shared the good news with everyone that it looked like the storm had cleared. She suggested to the group that Hogan might be better off staying there in the cabin, so he wouldn't have to be carried during their search. Angelo and Sam talked for a while and agreed that leaving water and food might be the best choice until they could get a chopper up to the area to pick him up.

5

ON THE ROCKS

The group gathered their belongings and ensured they loaded their weapons. Angelo reached the command center by walkie-talkie and informed the lieutenant about the discovery of the two bodies. Cache laid out a map on the table and Angelo advised the lieutenant of the last known position of the bodies. He shared their encounter with the wolves and said he couldn't guarantee that the bodies would still be intact if they were out foraging for food. The base command told them that they would send a team to the position to investigate the remains. As the storm had cleared the area, the priority had shifted to finding the escaped prisoners.

During the entire evening, as the group had sat around the fire, Cache had never been able to get some private time with Angelo to discuss what she'd found. She suggested they stay in the same teams today, to provide her with the opportunity to show him the paper she'd found on Terry Bolden.

After a breakfast of protein bars, dehydrated food and what resembled coffee, the team made their way out of the cabin at eight fifteen a.m. The command center had assured Sam that they would send a team up to the cabin to pick up Hogan as soon as they could get a helicopter in the air. The plan that morning was simple. The four of them would hike to the cabin closest to their position to see if Leo Bolden and his companion had made it there during the storm. From there Sam and Regan would push farther west to the Myers hunting cabin while Cache and Angelo made their way up the mountain. The Shellington cabin was about thirty minutes west of the Henderson cabin, and without the presence of intense falling snow, there was little that should slow their progress that morning. As Cache walked with the group, she found a few minutes where she was walking beside Angelo and she passed him the paper that she'd found on Terry Bolden. Angelo glanced at it and put it into his jacket pocket.

"Any idea what it means?"

"Nope, but the first names aren't that common. Who calls their kid Grover these days?"

Angelo scratched the back of his neck and surveyed the area, looking for signs of life. The morning was bright with the sun reflecting off of the snow.

"What do you think their chances were?" he asked Cache.

"In these parts, with that storm, if they didn't find shelter, this won't be a search but a recovery mission."

"These are the only cabins they could have found shelter in?"

"Only ones I'm aware of. The alternative would be to find shelter in one of the caves, but you'd risk encountering prior occupants that might not take kindly to your visit."

As they approached the cabin of Arthur Shellington, Sam and Regan took the forward position, with Cache and

Angelo covering the rear flank. Sam lifted his arm to signal for all of them to stop. Sam pointed out that there seemed to be a lot of footprints in the snow out in front of the cabin. Cache decided to have a look from the other side and moved around the exterior of the cabin. She could see footprints in the snow going along the side, with a set of prints going west toward the Myers cabin and a set going southeast back toward the area where the bodies of Terry and Doug lay in the snow. Cache rejoined the group, and they kneeled down to be less visible from the cabin. They formulated a plan: Angelo and Cache would go around the back of the cabin while Regan and Sam breached the front door. They crept toward the front of the cabin, alert for any signs of life. When all were in position, Sam put his shoulder to the door and gripped the door handle. Regan stood on the other side of the doorway, weapon drawn, with both hands on the grip. Sam turned the door handle and pushed in with his shoulder.

"You're under arrest," he yelled, drawing his weapon as Regan followed in behind him. But the cabin was deserted. Regan walked out to the front of the cabin and yelled for the others to join them inside.

The four of them walked around the cabin and noted points of interest. The cabin comprised three rooms: a small bedroom in the back, a small kitchen and then a sitting area in front of the fireplace. Cache moved to the bedroom and searched the room. The bed was unmade—not like Arthur Shellington; those who knew him well knew he was a stickler for being tidy. Cache poked her head out of the bedroom. "Someone was sleeping in this bed." She looked around the bedroom. A few long strands of red hair were on one of the two pillows. The dresser drawers were ajar, and a closer examination showed that someone had rummaged through them. She got down on her knees and looked under the bed, where she found a pair of black rubber boots size large. She walked out of the bedroom holding the boots in her hands. "Found these." The others didn't seem to be impressed, dismissing them as likely the cabin owner's property. Regan searched the fireplace; the ash was still warm. Sam searched through the kitchen and found evidence that someone had been through the cabinets. Angelo sat in the main sitting area, watching everyone poke around the small cabin.

"So, what do you think? Leo and companion or Fleming brothers?"

"Based on the red hair found on the pillow, my guess is Leo and companion. Must have made it here to seek shelter from the storm. And then there are these." Cache sat down near Angelo, holding the rubber boots in the air.

"Yeah, so what?" Regan said as he sat down near Cache.

"You don't know Arthur. There is no way he would wear bargain rubber boots—you see here? The price tag is still on. No, Arthur takes a lot of ribbing from my dad because he insists on wearing expensive hiking boots." Cache turned the boots over and noticed the L symbol on the bottom. "These are size large; Arthur would wear a medium, he's not that tall."

"Yeah, but Leo is not tall either. Terry was over six feet, Leo five foot four; he wouldn't wear size large either," Angelo said.

Sam reached out to take the boots from Cache. "You know, both the Fleming brothers are big guys. They would wear a size large; maybe they're theirs."

"That could mean all four of them were here in the cabin last night," Cache said, "or they could be the redhead's."

"Well, they're not here now. Any suggestions?" Angelo asked.

"There are two sets of tracks out back. One goes west-ward, and one goes south."

"Okay, so Cache and I will continue westward. it would make sense for Leo to get out of the area as soon as possible; going south now that the storm has let up means they would run into more people like us, but we need to check it out. Sam, you and Regan take the southern route; you might also run into the forensics team."

As they were preparing to leave, something caught Angelo's eye by the door. He reached over to pick up the objects on the floor. "Spent bullet cartridges. Someone was doing some shooting. Sam, can you find something in the kitchen I can wrap these up in?" Sam went to the kitchen and returned with an old ragged tea towel that he put the spent cartridges in and tucked them into his jacket. The four of them got up and left the cabin. Cache and Angelo followed the trail to the west as Regan and Sam headed southward.

The snow was still deep, and each step proved a chal-lenge, but the snow had stopped falling, and that reduced one of Mother Nature's obstacles.

"Angelo, can I ask you something?"

"Sure."

"Does Sam know Nancy Milne well?"

"I don't think he knows her at all, but it's a small commu-nity, you never know. Why?"

"Just curious. Another one for you."

"Shoot."

"If the Fleming brothers are up here looking for the Boldens, why is her husband not up here?"

"Another good question. I don't have the answer to that one. Now, I have a question for you."

"Okay."

"What are you doing here?"

"You hired me."

"I recognize I hired you. Why aren't you off playing house with some mister somewhere instead of being out here with the likes of us?"

Cache clenched her jaw. If she had been one of her brothers, would the same question have come up?

"I was in the army for years, miss it every now and again, and thought this might rekindle some memories."

"Thinking about going back?"

"Some days, just feeling restless, like I should do something bigger with my life. I thought I would work on the ranch, but now I don't know."

"That's the Iron and Sons ranch? I guess you don't count."

"Sometimes it feels that way. My great-grandfather founded the ranch when he moved to Montana. He just had sons. In four generations, I was the first daughter born to the family. My mother attributes it to strong Cooper blood."

"So why doesn't your family change the name?"

"They rationalize that it's been that way so long that to change it would be wrong."

As the two walked farther west, they were spending the time getting to know each other better when something blue in the distance caught Cache's eye. They approached cautiously, guns drawn, until they reach a mound of snow with something blue underneath. Cache reached her hand down into the snowbank, grabbed on to something and hoisted it out of the snow. The body of a man in his thirties, wearing black pants and a blue jacket, came out from under the pile of snow. Cache laid him on his back. He had a black beard and brown eyes with a noticeable bullet hole in the front of his forehead. Angelo patted the body down and unzipped his jacket to search his pockets. He located a wallet that identified the body as one Norm Fleming. They moved him onto his side, where Cache noted two bullet holes in the back of his right leg. They let the body fall back onto its back. Cache put her fingers against his skin; the body still felt warm.

"So, this might have happened recently."

They scanned the area and noticed a single set of footprints moving away from the body; instead of continuing westward, they seemed to veer off and move south. They searched his remains and gathered what personal effects he had. His wallet contained only identification. Whoever had done this must have taken his cash and credit cards, if there had been any. Cache accessed their GPS position from her smartphone and Angelo called in to police command, telling them to get a team up here and examine the remains.

———

Cache and Angelo continued on their trek, following the single set of footprints from much smaller feet, moving in a southward direction, toward where Regan and Sam were canvassing the terrain. Angelo grabbed his walkie-talkie.

"Sam, Regan, you there? Come in if you can hear me."

"Yeah, we can hear you, over," said Sam.

"We found the body of Norm Fleming, two bullet wounds to the back and a fatal shot to the head. The remaining trail appears to be heading south, so we may come across you at some point. Have you had any luck?"

"Yeah, I can say with confidence our manhunt is over."

"You captured Leo Bolden?" Angelo asked.

"Nope, my guess is he came in contact with whoever shot your victim. We found him a short time ago, wedged into a group of rocks, one bullet wound to the head. No sign of anyone else in the area. He has bite marks on different parts of his torso, so we don't know how long he's been dead. Regan is on his phone with the command center."

Angelo looked up at Cache. "Well, that ends our manhunt."

"Yeah, but we have four bodies and no shooter. Ask them if they found anything on the body?"

"Sam, did you find anything on the body?"

"Nope, picked clean, just clothes similar to what Terry was wearing. Is Cache with you?"

"Yeah, I'm here, Sam."

"Curious thing, Leo is wearing large rubber boots, an exact match for the ones you found in the cabin."

"Okay, we're heading toward you. The tracks going westward have now changed direction. Send me your GPS position and we'll see you shortly," Angelo said.

Cache and Angelo continued on the journey southward. The snow remained deep in some places and lighter in others. The footprints in the snow were from smaller-sized feet. Cache reflected that there had been no sound of gunfire that morning. While the shots could have come from a distance off, any loud noise would have echoed in the area with the rocks and trees, and by all accounts they were not far off from the GPS coordinates that Sam had sent over. They continued south for about twenty minutes, until they came to a clearing with pine trees to their left and a formation of rocks and trees to their right.

The snow showed multiple sets of prints and large indentations in the snow; it was impossible to determine what direction the people who'd made them had come from and which way they'd left the area. As they stood in the clearing, Angelo picked up his walkie-talkie to contact the command center. Cache surveyed the area with her binoculars and noticed something in the rocks, something red that appeared to be moving. She realized that while the snow had stopped, there was still a wind in the area. The rocks had caught something on their jagged edges and the wind was likely moving it back and forth.

She turned to Angelo and told him she would be back in a few minutes. He likely thought she was just going somewhere private because nature was calling, but she moved to her left and walked in among the pine trees. From there she took her rifle off her shoulder, clutched it in her hands, kneeled down in the snow, moved around the trees to the base of the rock formation and made her way up the hill to come out above the area where she'd identified the red object. As she reached the top of the hill, she could see Angelo in the clearing still talking on his walkie-talkie. She scanned the rocks and noticed that the red item she had spotted belonged to a red jacket being worn by what appeared to be a man, hiding in the rock formation. He kept glancing about from side to side, likely trying to determine where Cache had gone. She crept down the hill, bracing herself against the rocks and slithering like a snake closer to the hidden individual until she was behind him.

She pressed the end of her barrel into the back of the stranger's head.

"Move an inch, and the view you're seeing is the last view you will ever see. Understood?"

The figure nodded.

"I would prefer something more audible so there is no confusion."

The stranger said in a husky voice, "Understood."

"Okay, now we will stand up and move down the hill to my friend down there."

They slowly stood up from the rocks and began moving toward Angelo. Angelo at first didn't react, until he saw Cache leading a stranger to him, and then he quickly drew his service weapon.

"He was watching us in the rocks. Thought we should get to know one another." Cache pulled down the hood of the man's jacket to reveal his face.

"Hey, Kyle, fancy running into you here," Angelo said.

"Oh, thank god it's you, Malone, I was afraid this one was her," he said as he motioned with his thumb to point behind him.

"Who, Cache? She's with me. Who did you think she was?"

"Norm and I caught sight of a woman this morning at the Shellington cabin, knew that wasn't old man Shellington."

"What did she look like?"

He turned to look at Cache. "Any chance you can put the rifle down?" Angelo motioned with his hand for Cache to lower her weapon.

"Did she look like her?"

"Kind of hard to tell with the face mask on."

Cache pulled her thermal face mask off and looked at Kyle.

"Nah, the one we spotted had long red hair, black leather jacket, tight pants on. Did not seem like she belonged in the woods during the storm."

"So, did you say hello? Maybe she needed help."

"Probably should have, but everything happened so fast."

"What did you do, Kyle?"

"Norm and I decided that we would bust in to surprise her. After all, we were looking for someone and thought she might know something."

"Wouldn't have been Terry and Leo Bolden, would it?"

Kyle just stood there in silence, looking at Angelo. He realized Angelo knew they were not just out hunting rabbit.

"We have a score to settle with them, and you know why."

"Well, go on. You bust into the cabin, probably scaring the poor woman to death ..."

"Yeah, she didn't appear too scared. Pulled out a pistol and started firing at us. Norm grabbed a small bag that she had on the table and we hightailed it out of there."

"Then what happened?"

"As we were running, Norm was looking through the bag and didn't see much. Found a piece of paper and looked at it and handed it to me. Then we noticed that she was running after us in the snow, stopping to fire at us. Norm headed toward the Myers cabin and I headed south. We were going to meet up down near the highway where we parked on the side of the road."

"Where is the bag now?" Angelo asked.

"My brother Norm's got it."

"Afraid not," Cache said.

"What do you mean?"

"We found Norm dead in the snow. No bag was with him. Then we found tracks heading south. My guess is she came this way looking for you."

"Norm's dead! Oh my god, what am I going to tell his wife and my parents?" He just fell down in the snow, holding his hands to his eyes, and sobbed.

Angelo kneeled down beside him. "Look, I'm sorry, but

you guys had no business being out here, you should have just let us handle it."

Cache and Angelo stepped away and allowed some time to pass while Kyle processed the news about his brother. Angelo radioed command that they had Kyle Fleming with them and that they would head to the location of Leo Bolden's body. He would ask Sam to escort Kyle safely out of the area and back to the command post to give a statement and answer questions. Angelo walked over to Kyle and crouched down in the snow.

"I need you to come with us. We're meeting two other officers and one of them will take you back to the command post, where we will have some questions for you. The piece of paper that you mentioned, do you still have it?"

Kyle reached into his pocket and gave the small piece of paper to Angelo. Angelo flipped it open and noticed the torn edge at the bottom. He reached into his jacket pocket, got the piece of paper that Cache had found on Terry Bolden and lined up the torn edges. They were a perfect match. He handed the paper pieces to Cache.

"Two pieces of paper and two brothers. What do you bet this top piece came from Leo?"

"You think Leo gave her the paper?" Kyle asked.

"Possibly."

Cache handed the pieces of paper back to Angelo for safekeeping. They helped Kyle up and walked toward the area that matched the GPS coordinates Sam had sent. When they were about fifteen minutes from the location, they stopped, and Angelo took Cache to the side to whisper in her ear.

"He doesn't appreciate that we realize Leo and Terry are dead, and I want to keep it that way, in the event he had something do with it."

"What do you want to do?" Cache asked.

"Can you go fetch Sam and tell him to come this way? I'll stay here with Kyle, that way he doesn't see us near the body."

Cache walked off toward Sam and Regan until she happened onto the two of them near a formation of rocks. The body of Leo Bolden was wedged between the rocks, his hair blowing in the wind, showing no other sign of movement.

"Hey, Angelo doesn't want Kyle to know that we know Terry and Leo are dead, so he's waiting for you about fifteen minutes in that direction," she said as she pointed in the direction she'd come from. "What's Regan doing?" she asked as she looked over at Regan, who was just staring down at the body of Leo Bolden.

"Odd thing; he took Leo's hat off his head and has just been staring at him. I had to search the body. He didn't want to have anything to do with it. Not much of a detective, if you ask me."

"Hey, any word on Hogan?" Cache asked.

"Yeah, chopper picked him up about half an hour after we left. The local vet will examine him."

Sam left the area, heading toward Angelo and Kyle, as Cache walked over to Regan.

"You okay?"

"Why wouldn't I be? Just a criminal who met justice."

"Sam thought—"

"Let's not worry about what Sam thought. Did you get anything from Kyle?"

"Yeah, apparently there is a redhead in the area who likes to shoot people."

6

RED LIES

Angelo joined Cache and Regan near the body of Leo Bolden.

"What are your thoughts?" he asked Regan.

"There is no mistaking the cause of death; a bullet to the head will do that to you. What are you thinking?"

"We have a woman with long red hair, wearing a black leather jacket, carrying a weapon that she seems to know how to use. Based on what Kyle said, we suspect that she killed Norm Fleming and was looking for Kyle Fleming when we found him."

"Why would she be out here in this weather looking for the Fleming brothers? You can find them any Friday night at Shady Stu's pub."

"Shady Stu's?" Cache asked.

"It's a bar in Quinn that they like to frequent. I've gone in there now and again and spotted them at the bar talking up the female bartender."

Angelo looked at Leo Bolden and sighed. "Well, Cache, we hired you to help us find these two; now it looks like you're off the clock."

"Do you want to head back in? I'll buy you a cup of coffee," Cache said.

"I think we need to finish our job. We'll have the chopper fly over the area and see if they can spot our mystery woman from the air. Regan, you up for having a look for her?"

"Yeah, let's find this bitch."

Cache shook the hands of both of them and told them it had been a pleasure to be in their company. For Angelo, she meant it; for Regan, she was just being nice. She headed south toward the snowmobiles they had parked yesterday. Regan and Angelo split up, with Angelo heading back toward the Shellington cabin, where the redhead had stayed the night, and Regan heading toward the Henderson cabin to see if there was anything that they had missed.

Cache had walked for a few miles when something occurred to her. She walked back to the location where Leo Bolden's body lay among the rocks and stared at him for a few minutes. Cache examined the body's position. She studied his facial features, dark hair, cleft chin, a small scar above the right eye. Something about him bothered her, but she couldn't put her finger on what. After a few minutes of reflection, the thought of a hot bath sounded good, and she made her way to the parked snowmobiles.

———

Regan walked for about twenty minutes and grabbed his phone to pass the time. He seemed unconcerned about wild animals in the area and more interested in seeing what he'd missed on social media in the past twenty-four hours. As he walked around a bend thick with pine trees, he didn't notice the long-legged redhead sitting on a rock about twenty feet ahead of him with an automatic handgun with silencer gripped in her left hand.

"Where do you think you're going, Michael?"

Regan froze in the snow and put his hands in his pockets. He looked at her as she got off the rocks and walked toward him, pointing a gun at him. She walked until the silencer was about a foot away from his chest, when he reached out and grabbed her left hand and pulled her in close. Their mouths engaged; he tasted her cherry-flavored lipstick and sniffed the faint scent of roses from her neck, and he pulled out his other hand and planted it around her waist.

"Hannah, I've been worried about you being out here with those two."

"A girl can take care of herself."

"It's not safe for us to be talking out here, there are choppers flying overhead trying to get a glimpse of us. There's a cabin about fifteen minutes away from here that way." He gestured in the direction in which he thought it lay. "Meet me there, and put your hood up."

"Can't we go together?"

"No, too dangerous."

Hannah walked off in one direction as Regan made his way toward the cabin on his original path. Regan reached the cabin before Hannah and surveyed the area to ensure there was no one else around. A police chopper had flown overhead as Regan waved to it and talked to them on his cell phone, telling them the area appeared to be clear and they should focus their search westward. He went inside the cabin and organized the surroundings. Regan grabbed three logs that Cache had stored close to the fireplace and started a fire using the lighter he carried in his pocket. He glanced around the room, reached into his pocket and found his police badge. Wouldn't do for her to learn that he was a cop, so he walked over to the kitchen and stored it in one of the upper cabinets beside some coffee mugs. He glanced down at his left hand. His wedding ring was glimmering as it reflected the flames coming from the fireplace. Another thing she didn't need to know about. He looked around the room for a place to hide it but couldn't find a suitable location and didn't want to lose it, to avoid the questions he would face when he got back home. He reached into the cupboard and pulled down a coffee mug from the top shelf. This should provide a safe storage place. He returned it to the top shelf. The last item to hide was his gun. He checked the clip to make sure it was full and tucked it under the mattress for the upper bunk bed. Regan was turning off his cell phone so they wouldn't be disturbed when a knock came from the door. He worried that other police officers were in the area and wondered how he could get rid of them so he could have some quiet time with Hannah.

"Hello, who's there?"

"The best time you'll have today."

The door swung open and Hannah O'Conner waltzed into the cabin. She looked at Regan and glanced over at the bunk beds. "I bet we could have fun in those."

"I'm sure we could break a few springs," he said.

She walked over to him, put her arms around him and planted her lips against his. Hannah could taste the cigarette he'd had a short time ago. His scent was musky—he needed a hot shower, one where she could join him—and the only sounds she heard were the crackling of the fire and his breath. She reached down and stroked the inside of his leg with her hand. "How I have missed that."

"Sorry about that—sorry about a few things."

"God, I wanted you to call me, even if it was only for you to come over and fuck me; you didn't have to stay. You could have grabbed me off of the street, dragged me into an alley and screwed me up against the wall. I just wanted to feel your touch."

"I suspect they were watching you."

"The police?"

"More than likely. The boys never divulged the place where they hid the money, and a couple of million dollars was sitting out there somewhere; they weren't just going to give up on that, you know."

She glanced over at the bunk beds.

"Do you want to screw me on the top one first?"

"No screwing today, sweetheart," he said as he brushed her hair from her face. "You have the most magnificent green eyes, they look like the greens at a golf course."

"Just what every woman wants to hear, they remind their lover of golf. We'll have a quickie. You can take me from behind; you used to like to bend me over all sorts of things before he came along."

"He didn't come along by accident."

"I know he was your chosen one, but might you have found someone nicer to screw your girlfriend?"

Regan moved his hand from Hannah's waist to rest it firmly on her ass as he pulled her in close to him. "Baby, there is a beach with our name on it. You won't be wearing clothes for a month."

She pushed away from him and roamed around the cabin. Hannah walked over to the fireplace, took off her gloves and unzipped her jacket and threw them over the chair. She stood in front of the roaring fire and warmed her hands.

"At least you have a fire. I found a cabin last night, sat in the dark as the storm raged on. Where did you stay?"

"Here; found this in the storm. Luckily, I could get the door open."

"What are you doing here?" she asked. "The plan was that I was to get the information from the boys and meet you back at my place."

"I know, but the thought of you out in a storm with them caused me concern and I came to look for you, to see if we could put an end to this once and for all. You mean everything to me. Damn the plan, I just wanted to know you were safe."

Hannah walked around toward the kitchen and noticed a lot of plates in the sink and coffee mugs on the counter. She pulled open a few drawers and opened the cabinets to see what was lurking inside.

"Did you have company last night?" she asked.

Regan glanced at the plates and mugs. "The owner must have left them out. Didn't see any reason to be his housekeeper."

She walked around the room and sat down on the lower bunk. She stretched out, put her head down on the pillow and looked at the bunk above. There was a strange impression underneath the mattress. Then she looked back at him. He had her backpack in hand and was looking through it. The first thing he removed and put on the table was an automatic handgun with silencer. He then pulled out additional clips and rounds.

"At least you were armed. It can be dangerous this far into the backcountry. Aren't you glad I taught you how to shoot?"

He continued to rummage through her bag: clothes,

food, water and two pair of handcuffs. As Regan held the handcuffs up, he asked, "What are these for?"

"I took them off those corrections officers, thought they might come in handy. The first one didn't know what hit him. Sat behind the wheel of the bus while the other left to see if he could help me out with my so-called engine problem. Even let me stand inside out of the elements. He looked like a nice guy, so I made it quick. He never saw it coming. Just pulled it out—didn't think twice—and squeezed the trigger. The sight of me popping off that guard seemed to get Terry horny, and that was something I had had enough of."

She sat up on the bed and pulled her boots off. "I felt sorry for the first guy but not the second. He eyed me up and down like I would give him a blow job right after he fixed my car. I stepped off the bus, when he got close enough, and popped two right into him. Hopefully it was good for him, because it was good for me."

"Sorry it had to be that way, but Terry and Leo looked like they would never give up the location of the money to you. Not when they were robbing the banks, not during your visits to the prison. Even when you stopped going to see Terry and told him you were moving on, that you couldn't afford to wait for him, he told you nothing. Then the brainless wonder decided breaking out of prison was a good way to go and screwed that up. He was a screwup his entire life."

That last statement raised Hannah's eyebrows. "I thought you only met Terry in his twenties."

"Yeah, just a figure of speech. So did they tell you anything?"

"Terry only told me how bad he wanted to fuck me. Leo had more questions than answers."

"Like what?"

"Like how did I know they were being transferred that day and how did I organize all of this."

"What did you tell him?"

"I told him I was screwing one of the prison guards and he let it slip during foreplay."

"Did he buy it?"

"I don't know."

Hannah glanced back over at the mugs on the counter. Something about the image was not sitting right with her. She noticed the ax against the fireplace, wood chips on the blade.

"Did you cut the wood for the fire?"

"Nah, the owner had a stack of logs next to the fireplace."

"My cabin didn't have any wood, so I just crawled into bed to stay warm."

Regan glanced down at her boots, which were lying on the floor, and noticed the name "Arthur" stitched across the side.

"Who is Arthur?" he asked.

Hannah glanced down to where he was looking and noticed the name on the boots for the first time. "Don't know. They were in the cabin and looked a lot more practical than the rubber boots I was wearing; they were too big for me. Remember, the plan was to drive somewhere out of state. Find out where they hid the money and then deal with them, call a tip line and send them back to prison. Terry insisted on driving, hit a patch of ice and sent us into the ditch. From there the weather forced us to go on foot; either we walked along the side of the road and waited for the police to find us, or we tried to survive in the backcountry.

"Then he just complained continuously about how I had stolen the wrong car and that I should have stolen something with better tires."

Regan laughed at the thought of Terry's going on and on, not being grateful that he was free. He pulled his chair in closer to Hannah, reached down for her feet and pulled them up on his lap. He rubbed them. Hannah always responded well to a good foot rub. She had been a waitress in a small truck stop when they first met. Her average day had her spending ten hours or more on her feet. It was that slight gesture that had made her fall for him. "Why did you guys separate? Why not stay together?"

"Terry was just berating me the whole time, like everything bad for him happened because of me. Man, I'd just killed two people to get him out of jail. It was just like when we were together; he was always putting me down, telling me what was wrong with me. I'm sorry, I just lost it; I left. The snow was coming down so heavy that after a few feet I couldn't see them. Leo came after me and we were on our own for the next several hours."

As he dug his thumbs into the balls of her feet, she twisted her neck from side to side. "That's a little too hard," she said. Regan continued to press hard and didn't let up. She had let her emotions get the better of her.

"You know you stood a better chance of getting the info out of them if the two of them stayed together."

She continued to roll her head from side to side. "What do you care how I did it? I got the info."

Regan stopped rubbing her feet. "You got, you got the info?"

She leaned back on her elbows and stared at him. "Of course I got it, but we have a bit of work to do first."

"Well, let me have it."

"Well, I don't have it, but I know where it is and how we can get it."

"Hannah, I don't like riddles. What are you talking about?"

She sat up straight and pulled her feet away from Regan. "Leo had scribbled the details down on a piece of paper. As we walked in the woods trying to keep an eye out for Terry, the police and any wild animals, he apologized for his brother's behavior all these years.

"I told him what hurt most of all, with everything I had done for them, was that they still didn't trust me. That seemed to be the trigger. He reached down into his pocket and pulled out a half-torn piece of paper. At the top was the name of a cemetery near Quinn called Greenwood."

Regan leaned back on his chair, braced himself by extending his feet against the bed and pushed back on the back two legs of the chair. He scratched his head and then his beard, and thought to himself that a cemetery would be the ideal place to hide money. People only visit so often, and Greenwood was an older frontier cemetery. They had buried no one in there for years. Its only visitors were probably historians. Judges were funny about granting a warrant to exhume a body unless you had tons of evidence, so the money could stay there for years undisturbed.

"I know Greenwood, but there has to be about sixty people buried there. They buried the money a few years ago, so any disturbed ground will have grass growing and it could be difficult to determine which grave the money is in. He didn't mention in whose grave they buried the money?"

"He had it written on the piece of paper. There were multiple names, and Terry had one half and Leo the other," she said.

"So we just need to find them and we have the names?"

"Leo gave me his piece of paper to hold, but then it was stolen."

"How did it get stolen?"

"This morning two guys busted into the cabin, grabbed the bag I had put the paper in and took off. They split up when I started chasing them and the guy with my bag must have given it to the other guy, because when I caught up with him he didn't have it."

"What makes you think he was telling you the truth?"

"I was the one holding the gun, and I checked for myself."

"So we need to find him or Terry and get the pieces of paper from them."

Hannah leaned forward on the bed and pulled her boots back on. "That's pretty much it." She got up to stretch her legs and walked over to the kitchen. "You didn't find anything to drink in this place, did you?" she asked.

Regan pointed to the cupboard to the right. "There is some whiskey in that cupboard over there."

Hannah walked over to the cupboard, found the whiskey and put it on the counter, then was poking around in the cupboards for a glass when she came across the mugs and noticed a thin black billfold tucked beside a coffee mug. She pulled the billfold down and opened it up to see a silver police badge on the right-hand side with the words *Quinn Police Department* engraved at the top and the word *Detective* engraved at the bottom. Her hands shook as she tried to keep the billfold hidden from Michael's view and turned it around to read the name on the identification. It said *Detective Regan Fox* next to Michael's picture. She slowly closed the billfold and put it back where she'd found it, pulled down a coffee mug and closed the cupboard door. With her back still turned to him, she reached over for the whiskey, poured herself a shot and threw it back.

"You sure I can't get you one?" she asked as she turned around.

Regan stood there beside the bed, his automatic weapon in his hand. She glanced down at the table and saw her weapon had disappeared.

"I wish you hadn't found that."

"Found what?" she said as she surveyed the room. Her jacket was near the fireplace, her bag still sat on the table and Regan's jacket was closest to him.

"Sweetheart, you would always be a loose end I had to deal with. I just needed you to get me the information before we parted company."

"Didn't you love me? I thought you loved me," she said.

"I loved being with you, I loved the moments we had together, but am I in love with you? I'm afraid not; you were just the middleman or -woman that I needed."

"What, are you going to kill me? Michael, I'm the one that does the killing, you don't like to get your hands dirty, remember?"

"See, I can't bring you in. The moment that pretty little mouth of yours moves, it won't take them long to figure it out, and that is not good for me."

She assessed her options. The distance between them was not that far, and the likelihood of his missing was not that good. She thought, Oh god, I don't want to die.

A knock came from the door. "Hey, Regan, are you in there?"

Regan looked at the door. Hannah threw the coffee cup at his head and made contact with him, giving her just enough time to open the door, where a gray-haired man with a beard was standing.

She screamed, "Run! He'll kill us all!" to the man as she ran past him and as far from the cabin as her legs could take her. Angelo looked stunned as he looked at Regan and stepped inside to render help just before Regan lifted his arm and squeezed the trigger.

7

ANGELS GO TO HEAVEN

The commotion stunned Angelo as the bullet struck the metal door frame and ricocheted. His instinct was to be anywhere but there, and he headed in the same direction as the redhead, running as fast as he could behind her, then veered off to the left, going in a direction they had not yet explored. He was uncertain what had transpired, but the redheaded woman looked like the woman they were hunting for. Why was she not in handcuffs, and why had Regan turned his phone off? Angelo continued to run until he came upon a rock formation and took up a strategic position behind one rock. He reflected on what had just happened. Had she been trying to escape from the cabin, and he'd shot to try to capture her, or was that shot meant for him? As he had approached the cabin, he'd overheard two voices talking as if two friends were having a casual conversation. At first, he had considered the individuals might have been the cabin owners, and that was the reason for his knocking. He thought about the conversation that he'd partially overheard and was certain that there was something about love in it. He reached for his walkie-talkie, but it wasn't there. In his haste as he ran from the cabin, it must have gotten dislodged from his belt. "Looks like I'm on my own," he said to himself, and he took out his gun and peered around the rocks. Everything looked still, everything was silent, and then the sound of Regan's voice shattered the quiet.

"Angelo, are you out here? Are you okay? I didn't mean to shoot at you, I was trying to prevent her from getting away."

Angelo looked around from the rocks and spotted Regan crouching down, moving along the rocks with his weapon clutched in both hands.

"Hey, I know what it looks like, um, it was unprofessional. I mean, if you saw her, she was hot; I hoped I might be able to exchange sex for her freedom. Awful call on my part."

Angelo considered what he was saying. He had known Regan for years, and he had always been the type of guy to cheat on his wife if he had the chance, so what he said was plausible. He stood up and moved away from the position that provided him cover.

"Regan, don't shoot, let's talk this out," he said. As he moved away from the rocks and became visible to Regan, Regan lifted his weapon and fired two rounds at Angelo, hitting the rocks. Angelo dove for cover, landing on his right wrist and twisting it; he felt the pain pulsating up his right arm. He grabbed his weapon with his left hand and lifted his head just above the rocks. Regan had taken cover, and when Angelo thought he'd spotted him, he returned fire. He pondered. There was no mistake this time. No redheaded woman was standing next to him. Regan had meant those shots for him.

He grabbed his right wrist. It felt like someone was

pounding it with a hammer and wouldn't stop. He attempted to pick up his gun with his right hand, but tightening his hand around the grip sent searing pain up his arm. Angelo thought, That won't work, and he knew he shot better with his right hand than his left. He pushed himself back up against the rocks and peered around the edge. No sight line to where Regan had positioned himself. He could circle around Angelo's position to get the drop on him. Angelo fumbled around in his jacket, looking for his cell phone. He looked at the battery-life bar and it was near dead; there had been no electrical outlets in the cabin and he'd never considered bringing a spare battery pack with him. Reception was down to one bar as he called the command post. Angelo felt his life was in danger and command needed to know there was something up with Regan. The phone rang and rang with no one picking up, and then it cut out. Again and again he pressed the power button, but his phone was dead. He didn't like where this was going; he had no way to reach anyone, he would have to shoot with his left hand and an officer wanted him dead for some unknown reason.

Angelo pushed himself up against the rocks. The area he'd come from was open, and Regan might easily pick him off if he went in that direction. He looked at the rocks to the left of him; they continued down a ways and then seemed to vanish from sight. He walked down the area, being careful with his footing. After a few feet, it was evident that he was on an incline. He walked down the rocky path sideways, putting more weight on his right foot and then his left, leaving his left hand in position to shoot in front of him if the situation called for it. Step by step he moved down the incline, the snow giving way to a flat, smooth rock surface as he put his foot down. He saw a continuous snow-covered path taking him down the side of the mountain. Angelo hadn't realized how far the Henderson cabin was up on Saugeen Mountain when he ventured out from it. He wished he had taken the path of the redheaded woman. He could have made his way down to the snowmobiles and retreated to the command post, where reinforcements would be. He looked up at the sky; it was clear blue with few clouds, and the sun bounced its rays of light off the snow in all directions. He thought, Why are there no choppers in the air? If I could find one and flag it down, it would get me to safety or prevent Regan from approaching any closer. Then he realized that someone on the ground apparently coming to his rescue might not seem like a bad thing to the pilot, as he had no way of informing them of what was going on.

He only had a few months left before he was handing in his badge and heading off to California to start his days of retirement, and now he feared that his life might end this very day in the back hills of Montana. No days at the beach, no sunsets to watch, just a snow-covered grave that might never be found. He kept moving down the hill step by step until his left foot couldn't find traction on the slippery rocks and he came crashing down on his right knee and slid down the rocky face, gaining speed the farther down he went. Angelo dropped his gun in a snowbank as he flailed his arms around in all directions, desperate to grab on to something to help slow his decent. He fell onto his back and put his heels down into the snow against the rock to try to get a grip, but there was nothing to get a grip on. It was like running on a sheet of ice; Angelo had no traction. He grabbed at the rock's edges as he moved quicker and quicker to an uncertain fate. With each grab, rock came loose and crumbled in his hand. He grabbed in all directions until he saw what looked like a drop ahead of him. As his legs slid past the edge of the cliff into open air, he made one final grab at some rocks on the edge with both his hands. He screamed with pain as his right hand caught hold of something and he came to a stop, with his knees dangling over the face of the rocks.

He grabbed the rock edge with his left hand and tried to hoist himself forward. Angelo moved about a foot up but he realized he was now in a precarious position. He looked at the rock face above him. There was a path of gray stone where the snow had come loose as he slid his way down the mountain. Climbing back up with an injured wrist would be tricky, and if he lost his grip, he would slide off the ledge into something unknown below. He tried to bring his breathing under control, taking deep breaths to try to calm himself down so he could think. If Regan came along the path, all he would have to do was slide something down to dislodge Angelo from where his body rested. To anyone else, it would look like an accident that had taken place in the backcountry. His retirement was something he was counting down to; he would not die here, not today, but he needed a plan, and that seemed lacking at the moment.

———

Regan walked along the rocks, being methodical about where he planted each step, careful so as not to alert Angelo to his position. He looked around at the area where he thought Angelo had run to but didn't see him anywhere. Did he go in a different direction? Could he be flanking me? Regan looked in all directions and noticed no sign of him. Years of planning the perfect crime, only to get lost in the minor details. He analyzed the situation from all the angles. If Angelo reached the command post and told his story,

Regan figured he would say that he had used poor judgement in trying to coerce a sexual relationship with the woman but Angelo was mistaken about the other details. That he was trying to apprehend the woman they were looking for and subsequent shots at him had originated from her. After all, he had been clever enough to take her gun and was using it now as he hunted Angelo down. She'd purchased it, though he'd told her where to go. If there were any fingerprints on the gun, they would be hers, as he had put his gloves back on before he searched her bag to ensure there were no traces of his fingerprints. If Hannah reached the command post, she was a suspected accomplice in the Bolden brothers' prison break. It would be her word against his. A well-known, well-liked detective, or so he thought.

No, he figured he had worked out the angles, but of the two of them, Angelo was more dangerous to him than Hannah. People in the department respected Angelo, and anything he said would result in some investigation playing out. Regan did not want the force to look for any ties between him and Hannah. While he believed he had been careful enough to cover his tracks, he also knew that he couldn't be 100 percent certain that there wasn't a shoe out there waiting to drop. Hannah was a smart girl; she was a survivor. He'd recognized that from the first conversation they had together, as she waited on his table while fending off advances from old truck drivers in the booth across from him. Was it possible that she had some insurance policy on him she could pull out and damage any credibility he had with the department? His best case was to get rid of the two of them. Kill Angelo with her gun and then shoot her dead and leave the weapon in her hands.

He looked at the blue sky; no clouds in sight. What a beautiful day this had turned into compared with the weather over the past few days. It gave him hope that today would be a new beginning for him once he finished up with a few details. He kept walking around the area where he had last spotted Angelo but didn't see any sign of him or any tracks in the snow.

"Ang, are you out here?" he yelled.

No answer came back. He knew Angelo wasn't stupid enough to respond, but it was worth a shot. After about thirty minutes of combing the area, he realized that he was going in circles. Tracks that he came across that he thought could be Angelo's, he soon realized, could also have been his. With all the movement going back and forth, it was becoming less and less likely that he'd be able to distinguish Angelo's tracks. He glanced down at his watch. He decided that he would turn his pursuit to Hannah and headed in the direction she had taken off in. She had about an hour on him, but the circumstances limited her options. Going south meant she could run into one of the other police teams they were sending into the area. Going north would require her to hike up the mountain, which she lacked the equipment for. No, she had two choices: either go west and continue on hoping to avoid the helicopter and ground units, or turn back and head east, which was the direction he was coming from. No more explanations, no more excuses. The moment he caught a view of that long red hair, he would add a few more spots of red to her cute little face.

Regan retraced his steps back to the cabin, keeping a watchful eye out for Angelo, Hannah or any other officers in the area. Other than the sets of tracks in the deep snow moving away from the cabin, there was no sign of life in the area. In his rush to leave the cabin and chase after Angelo, he had left two important items behind, his police badge and his wedding ring, and he didn't want to explain to various parties how or why he'd become separated from either of them. As he made his way to the front of the cabin, he noticed the front door was shut. He didn't recall closing the door as he raced out of the cabin. It hadn't seemed important at the time, given how essential it was to take care of Angelo and then Hannah. Since the door swung inward, it was always possible that a breeze had come down the stone chimney and blown the door shut, but there were no strong winds today. Perhaps Angelo had made his way back to the cabin and was waiting for him to open the door.

He walked around the cabin to the small window. Regan could see nothing through the dirty glass, as the fire was no longer providing light to the room. He walked to the front of the cabin and put his ear to the door to listen but heard nothing. He gripped his gun as he slowly turned the door handle with his left hand, pushed it open and walked in. Nobody was there. He looked around the room and noticed a few things were missing: Hannah's jacket and gloves, which she'd hung over the chair, and her black backpack, which he had left on the table. "That bitch," he said to himself. He walked over to the cupboard where he had hidden his badge, but it was no longer there. Regan looked around the cabin, opening and shutting drawers and cupboard doors. He searched the floor in the event she had flung it somewhere and the darkness now concealed the black billfold in the cabin, but he couldn't find it anywhere. At that moment, the hair on the back of his neck stood up as he gazed up at the cupboard where he'd hidden his badge. He got up and ran to it and grabbed for a coffee mug on the top shelf and pulled it down; empty. He repeated the process until the cupboard was bare. His wedding ring was gone. She must have found it when she came back for her things. How would he explain losing such an intimate item to both his wife and the members of the police command? This added a new wrinkle he might not be able to explain away. He had to get rid of her more than he needed to find Angelo. Only she knew what he had done, and if she shared her story with the world, then he might wear a set of orange coveralls for the rest of his life. He grabbed his backpack and tucked her pistol with its silencer down deep inside. He would need to kill her with his police-issued weapon to support the narrative that he'd shot her while she was trying to avoid arrest.

He headed out of the cabin and closed the door behind him. There was a trail going southeast from the cabin, which showed a smaller set of footprints with a shorter stride. This was definitely her path. Regan holstered his gun and ran along the path. He would need to maintain a quick pace if he stood any chance of catching her. The snow was deeper at some points than others, and he hoped this impediment might slow Hannah down and provide him with an opportunity to catch up. He covered a lot of ground in a short amount of time and found himself in a small area bordered by several large pine trees. As he came to a halt to catch his breath, he heard someone shout his name.

"Regan, Regan, over here."

He observed a man in a dark blue jacket who appeared to be Sam trudging through the snow.

Oh great, another one I have to put down, he thought as he pulled off his backpack and reached down to grab Hannah's gun, then realized Sam was not alone but accompanied by two other individuals dressed in white parkas and snow pants and shouldering black automatic rifles with white camouflage paint on the barrels and stocks. He put Hannah's pistol back in the bag and put the pack back on.

"Hey, Regan, why you here by yourself? Where's Angelo? We haven't been able to reach either of you."

"We caught sight of the redheaded woman and took off after her and got separated. Who are your friends?"

Sam introduced two members of the Montana National Guard who'd joined him in the search. Now multiple teams of the National Guard were involved in the hunt, with particular interest in finding him and Angelo. Sam explained that more choppers would be in the area in the next several hours, dropping soldiers in different strategic areas.

"Regan, don't worry, we will get her. She doesn't know it, but the net is getting smaller. We have teams coming in from three directions; it's only a matter of time."

"Sam, that is good to hear. She took a shot at us, so beware."

"Angelo found Norm Fleming and is convinced that she killed him over a piece of paper, so we won't hesitate to put her down if necessary."

"What piece of paper?" Regan asked.

"Something they found in a bag they stole from her. Norm and his brother grabbed it from her and hightailed it out of there. She must have figured Norm had it and killed him over it, when Kyle had it."

"Where is it now?" he asked.

"He was showing it to the debriefing team back at the command post. They're not sure what to make of it, it's just three names, but they'll run them through the database to see if they mean anything."

"Love to get a look at it myself."

"Detective Merjon has it now, so I would check with him."

"Oh, Greg's got it, yeah, I will check with him when I get

back in. You know, I came from this direction and was heading back toward the Henderson cabin to search for her. Why don't you and your friends look up that way. I'll double back this way"—he pointed in the direction he was originally heading in—"and see if I can find Angelo, and then maybe we'll head in."

Sam looked at the footprints in the snow moving away from them. "Are those hers?"

"No, I think they're Cache's; she must be back home by now."

"Hey, is your cell phone on?"

Regan knew the answer already but reached down into his pocket and pulled it out. "No, it's off, I think I was trying to conserve battery power."

"Well, turn it back on. If you catch sight of the redhead, let us know and we'll double back from our position and join you."

With that, Sam and the two guardsmen headed toward the Henderson cabin. Regan's pulse was racing. What more could go wrong? he thought.

8

RED REVELATIONS

Cache had been walking for about twenty minutes when she came to a stop. While she knew she had done the job they'd hired her for, she felt uneasy leaving Regan and Angelo to face the wilderness themselves. She pulled her face mask off and tucked it into her jacket. She then radioed into the command post for a status update and to try to get some sense of where Angelo and Regan might be located. The woman manning the communication center in the command post informed her that all attempts to reach either of the two men had been unsuccessful and there was some concern at command that something might have happened to them. Cache had just suggested that she might turn around and see if she could find either of them when Sam jumped on the radio.

"Hey, Cache, yeah, we can't reach either of them, when did you last spot them?"

"About twenty minutes ago, it's been quiet out here."

"You know, it's probably nothing; my cell phone was dead when I got back here, and they might be having similar issues. The batteries on their walkie-talkies could also be drained of power."

"Angelo said my job was done and suggested I head back, but I don't feel right leaving if something might be wrong."

"Please check things out. The National Guard is here and is being deployed, but you're still ahead of us by some distance."

"I'll head back and see if I can figure out what's going on and will call you if I learn anything."

Cache signed off with Sam and turned around and headed in the direction she had come from.

She walked back for about fifteen minutes, until she approached a group of pine trees. She observed the bend in the path and her footprints coming from that direction. As she turned around the bend, a flash of red came barreling at her and knocked her down to the ground, landing her on her back. She looked up and saw a figure in black with long red hair running in the direction she had come from. Cache looked up from her position, worried that a grizzly bear was in hot pursuit of the woman, and tightened her grip around the gun holstered to her belt. She breathed a quick sigh of relief when there was no sign of any wild animal giving chase, and she got to her feet and raced after the woman.

"Stop!" she yelled, but the woman would not heed her directions; she just kept on running.

As Cache gave chase, the woman was tiring, and Cache with each step was gaining more and more ground until it appeared the woman might be within arm's reach.

She looked back at Cache and said, "Please leave me alone."

In her effort to look behind her, she had lost valuable space between her and Cache. Cache looked at her black pants and tan hiking boots; pushed off with the balls of her feet, as if she were making a diving catch in the end zone of a pro football game; and grabbed the woman's pant leg. She then reached up, tucking her hand into the woman's waistband, and pulled down, exposing her posterior, the back of her legs and a bright neon-pink thong with black lace. The woman's tripping over her own feet caused her to come crashing down into the snow, which helped to absorb her fall.

She turned over on her back and kicked Cache in the ribs to push her off. Cache grabbed hold of her jacket and pulled herself forward as if she were pulling herself up into the saddle of a horse that didn't want to be ridden until she straddled the redheaded woman. The woman grabbed Cache by the hair and attempted to pull her off of her. Cache placed her left hand down on the top of the woman's chest to brace herself and backhanded her twice across the face. Little drops of blood spattered on the back of Cache's brown leather gloves as the redheaded woman's nose bled. Cache reached for her M9, grabbed the grip with both hands and pointed it in the face of the redheaded woman.

"At this range I won't miss."

Cache noticed the woman's lips quiver, and tears rolled down her face.

"Are you going to kill me? It might be better if you did," she said.

"If I was going to kill you, I wouldn't have chased you down, I would have dropped you from a ways off. Now I have a question for you: who are you?"

"Are you a cop?" she asked.

"Nope, a rancher."

"What the fuck, get off of me."

"Have you forgotten the gun pointing at your pretty face?

Lots of places around here to bury a body, or I just leave you wounded and the animals will look after you. They're hungry this time of year."

Hannah looked around and realized no one was coming to her rescue. If Regan found her, she would just as likely end up dead. She weighed her options in her head.

"Let's try this again: who are you?" Cache asked, stretching the words out for emphasis.

"How would you like a million dollars to let me go?"

"You have a million dollars on you?"

"Well, no, but I have a good idea where that amount might be."

"Yeah, so do I, it's called a bank."

"Banks have vaults and guards; where I'm talking has neither. You can go and get it, just let me go."

Cache pondered her offer for a few moments and didn't say a word.

"Sounds good, right? Get off of me and I'll tell you where it's at."

"You know, I thought about it. After federal taxes and the way the financial markets are these days, I would just lose it all and then feel sad about the whole thing. Who wants to be sad if they can help it?"

"Are you fucking nuts? You don't pay taxes on it."

Cache pushed the barrel of her gun up under the nose of the woman. "Let's try this one more time: who are you?"

"My name is Hannah." Cache felt they were now getting somewhere. By being able to address her by her first name, she might be able to establish a rapport with her.

"Hannah is a pretty name, do you have a last name that goes with the first?"

"O'Conner," she said.

"Oh, a wee bit of the Irish, I perceive, goes with the red

hair. I knew few Irish men in my time—good drinkers, lousy lovers." Despite the situation they found themselves in, Cache wanted to create a human connection with Hannah. "Okay, Hannah, so from what I have heard, you shot a few people, and they died. We don't like that in this state."

"Shot them with what? I don't have a gun."

"You could have ditched it, or it might be in your backpack."

"Search it, you're going to anyway."

"That doesn't mean you didn't throw it in a snowbank somewhere."

"Prove it."

Cache weighed her options. Without backup covering Hannah, there was a risk she could just bolt when Cache got up off of her, and she wanted to check her for weapons.

"Okay, Hannah, this is what we will do: I will sit up and you will roll over; you can rest your head on your hands so you're not facedown in the snow, and then I will check you for weapons and have a look in your backpack." Cache lifted herself off Hannah, helped roll her over and sat back down on her butt. She pulled the backpack off and set it aside as she patted Hannah down, ensuring there were no guns or knives hidden somewhere.

"Is it turning you on? If that's what you're interested in, perhaps we could go somewhere."

"Yeah, I'm sure you would be a lot of fun, but then you would sneak out and break my heart, and I would hunt you down and turn you into feed for our cattle," Cache said.

Cache reached over for the backpack, put it down on Hannah's back and opened up the flap. She moved things around inside, but sure enough, no guns or knives were spotted.

"You're right, no weapons."

"See, I told you. Now would you get off of me?"

"Not yet, honey." Cache continued to poke around inside the bag and found two pairs of handcuffs. "You're into some kind of kinky stuff, aren't you?" she asked.

Hannah didn't respond as she didn't want to admit where the handcuffs had come from.

Cache then found the gold wedding ring and pulled it out. She inspected it and saw the inscription was to Regan. Cache had a bad feeling in her stomach. How had this woman come into possession of Regan's wedding ring?

"Nice ring, is it yours?"

"My boyfriend's."

"Your boyfriend is married?"

"Yeah, turns out he was keeping it a secret—he was keeping a lot of secrets."

"So what did you do when you found out?"

"Threw a mug at him."

"Oh, I would have figured with that fiery temper redheads are supposed to have that you would have done a lot more."

"Would have, except . . ."

"Except what?" Cache asked, uncertain whether she wanted to hear the answer.

"He pulled a gun on me. He didn't want me saying anything to his wife or anyone else."

"Does this boyfriend have a name?"

"Michael, Michael Murphy, but that turned out not to be his actual name either."

Cache fumbled around in the bag and came in contact with the black billfold. She pulled it out and opened it up to reveal Regan's badge and police identification. Her initial feeling that something bad had happened with Regan disappeared with all the memories she had of his making it clear that he would hop into the sack with her the moment she said yes. She leaned forward and showed the picture portion of the identification to Hannah.

"Is this Michael?"

"Yeah, that's what he called himself. Never said he was a cop."

"Perhaps he was undercover trying to get information on the Bolden brothers."

"Cops don't plan the crimes. They do that, they'll take jobs away from the criminals."

Cache recognized this was serious but couldn't help but chuckle about the idea. She reached down into the bag and grabbed at one of the sets of handcuffs. Cache couldn't find a key anywhere in the bag or on Hannah and figured it might require bolt cutters to get these off of her, but they would serve to incapacitate her. She pulled Hannah's hands behind her back and handcuffed her wrists together.

"I will help you up, and then I want you to sit down and we will continue this conversation. You run, I shoot you, you fall down, got it?" Cache helped Hannah sit up and sat her down on top of her backpack so she wasn't sitting in the snow. Cache then sat down opposite her so they could talk face-to-face.

"Hannah, my name is Cache. I want you to tell me about this Michael."

"Where do you want me to start?"

"Tell me how you met."

"We met about seven years ago at Big Al's Truck Stop on Interstate 80, about an hour outside of Cheyenne."

"Not familiar with it. What was it like?"

"Typical truck stop, smelled of gas fumes most days, loud as rigs honked at one another either to say 'hello' or 'get out of my way.' Rumbling engines, people yelling at one another."

"Was there a diner there?"

"Yeah, that's where I worked. I waitressed there until a short while ago."

"Did you like waitressing?"

"It paid the bills. The owner let me park my motor home out back, that way I was close by if they got slammed with customers. The only thing I was qualified for, other than lying on my back."

"So how did you meet Michael?"

"One day, I was serving him coffee. He had this dreamy cleft in his chin before the beard. Several truckers in the next booth over were very curious what I had on under my skirt. They kept lifting it up to see what I was wearing underneath."

"That's terrible."

"Happened a lot, came with the job. Anyway Michael wasn't having any of it. He told them he was my boyfriend and that they would have to go outside with him if they continued. He is a big guy, and they didn't want to mess with him. First time anyone stood up for me. My dad left when I was two, and my mother never stood up for me, especially when her piece-of-trash boyfriends wanted to play with me in private. No, he was the first, and I knew he was the one."

Cache let her tell her story and would ask questions as she told it to ensure Hannah knew that Cache was listening to what she said. As the two talked about Hannah's early years, she became more comfortable with Cache and shared more information than she might have with the police if a lawyer had been present. Cache had spent years interrogating suspects when she was with the military police and brought all she had learned to this conversation with

Hannah. As Hannah shared her story, Cache sensed that this wasn't a line of bullshit but a factual account of some events that had led her here.

Michael had told her he was a salesman for a computer company and was on the road a lot, but whenever he found himself in Wyoming, he made time for her.

Cache could read her face as she shared intimate details of her relationship with Michael. It was clear to Cache that this woman was in love—not in lust but in love—with the man that Regan had pretended to be when he was with her.

As Cache tried to steer the conversation toward the Bolden brothers and any association Regan had with them, the speed at which Hannah would share things with her slowed down. Even though Regan had lied to her about important details, she still seemed resistant to sharing any particulars about how they had all ended up on the south side of Saugeen Mountain. Having grown up the way she had, she'd learned how to survive, and that instinct was in full force now. She wasn't prepared to say anything that could put her in jail, and Cache had no authority over her. Each time Cache brought the subject of the Bolden brothers up, she shut down, and Cache would steer the conversation back to when she and Regan were dating. She asked whether they talked about plans for the future and what they did when he would come into town, and then she would take another run at the Bolden brothers. It was like fighting with a fish that didn't want to be caught. Reel him in and then let him out, reel him in and then let him out, until he tires of the fight. That was what she was trying to do with Hannah, but Hannah was never prepared to set her foot into the bear trap.

Cache and she had been talking for more than a half hour when Cache did something unexpected and abandoned any further talk about the Bolden brothers. She would leave that to the police investigators who would need to read Hannah her rights and work to gather evidence for a court of law.

"Hannah, I wish I could let you go, I really do."

"Then do it."

"I can't. I respect the law too much. I need to turn you over to someone, but it won't be the man you call Michael. I don't know what is going on there, but I need to find a police sergeant; he will make sure you're safe while this gets figured out."

"So where is he?"

Cache looked from side to side. "He's somewhere out here. Maybe you caught sight of him in your travels: gray hair, gray beard, almost a sexy Santa Claus, but don't tell him I said that."

Hannah looked at Cache and didn't say a word. She knew who Cache was speaking of.

Cache could sense there was something wrong. Her eyes were no longer in direct contact with Cache's but more focused on the ground.

"Hannah, is there something wrong? Did I say something that upset you?" Cache asked. "Hannah, have you seen Angelo somewhere? We can't reach him on his cell phone or walkie-talkie."

She remained silent, just staring at the ground.

"Hannah, I am not a police officer anymore. When I hand you over, there is nothing I can do to help you. Angelo might help you, but I need to get you to him. If you know where he is, tell me."

"I don't know where he is."

"But you have seen him?"

"He caught me by surprise. I tried to warn him, but I needed to save myself."

"Warn him about what?"

"Michael was going to shoot me, probably didn't want his wife to know who else he had been sleeping with."

"How does Angelo come into all of this?"

"There was a knock at the door. It was the distraction I needed, so I threw my mug at Michael and opened the door. Your friend was there—at least I think it was him. I told him to run and then I left."

"What did he do?"

"I looked back, and he was following me. I was cold and scared and I could see Michael chasing after the two of us."

"Yeah, and . . . ?"

"I went one way, and when I looked back your friend wasn't behind me and I saw Michael running in a different direction."

"Then what did you do?"

"I stopped. I was freezing, I had left my coat and gloves back in the cabin. Man, if I hadn't put my boots back on, I would have been running in my socks through the snow."

"Hannah, stay with me. What happened to Angelo?"

"I really don't know. I stopped and waited to see if I could spot Michael, but there was no sign of him, so I returned to the cabin. I noticed footprints going off in a different direction but no sign of either man. So I snuck back to the cabin, where I stood in front of the fireplace for a few seconds to warm up. Then I threw my coat and gloves on and grabbed my bag."

"Was that it?"

"I had found his badge before he pointed a gun at me. I moved back to where I found it and grabbed it. I thought maybe I could use it as leverage somehow. As I was leaving, I wondered if there was anything else he had hidden. So I went through all the drawers, the cupboards, looked under the bunk beds, and then inside of a coffee mug I found the gold ring with the inscription to Regan, which matched the name on the identification for the man I knew as Michael."

"You said the cabin had bunk beds?"

"Yeah, tucked off to the side. Why does that matter?"

"It means the cabin you were in was the Henderson place and not the Shellington cabin."

Cache sensed that Angelo might be in trouble. She grabbed her cell phone, and the battery was near dead. She pulled off her backpack, reached inside one of the side pockets for a power bank and plugged her phone into it. The power bars glowed green as it charged the cell phone. She called Sam to see where he was.

"Sam, it's Cache, where are you?"

"We're just leaving the Henderson place. No sign of the redhead anywhere, why?"

"I have her here with me."

"You got her? Great, where are you?"

"Before I tell you, who are you with?"

"Two national guardsmen, why?"

"Regan is not with you?"

"No, we caught up to him, he was heading to the Shellington place to check the area out. Why?"

"I have a feeling Angelo might be in danger, but I think I might stand a better chance of finding him than you. I will email you my GPS coordinates. I need you to come get Hannah from me and take her back to the command post. Sam, whatever you do, don't let Regan near her. There is something between these two; I think it would be safer for her if you kept them apart."

After about a twenty-minute wait, Cache could see Sam

trudging along in the snow with two armed snowmen behind him. Cache introduced him to Hannah and told him she would call him if she found Angelo. With that, she grabbed her backpack and headed back up toward the Henderson cabin.

9

FALLING ROCKS

Cache ran as quickly as possible as the snow pushed her back with some resistance. The path to the cabin had been well traveled that day, and there was a path leading almost to the front door. As she approached the cabin, she grabbed her binoculars and panned them across the area, looking for another set of tracks. She spotted indentations in the snow heading to her right, and she plotted a course to intercept them. She ran as fast as she could but tired from trying to get through deep layers of snow. The fresh path took her into a rocky area with large gray boulders and pine trees sprouting up from behind them. She cupped her hands around her mouth and shouted, "Angelo, are you out here?"

The wilderness responded with silence, but the tracks continued until she reached a clearing where there were multiple tracks going in a variety of directions, with a set of tracks leading back in the direction from which she'd come. She thought, Is it possible that he made his way back and we missed each other in passing? She walked around in a circle, trying to make sense of the various footprints. The tracks were large but not animal-like, so they likely originated from a man, which disqualified Hannah from having made the tracks. She walked around in circles, following the prints, and came to rest at a rocky formation. Cache looked around, more confused than ever. She called Sam to ensure that Hannah had made it back to the command post okay. He confirmed that the trip back had been uneventful, and that there was no sign of Angelo or Regan back at command and people were growing concerned. The helicopter had run low on fuel and had gone back to the airport for refueling. It would be back in the area in about an hour, but with so much terrain to cover, it wasn't clear where they should begin.

Cache told Sam about the tracks leading out of the area she was in, and that it was possible Angelo might not even be in the area. She had four or five more hours of favorable light ahead of her and then she would be forced to seek shelter back at the Henderson cabin or to head back to the command post and venture out in the morning with Sam and the national guardsmen. She grabbed her canteen from her bag and sipped on the icy-cold water as she stared down at her feet. Then she noticed an odd set of tracks heading to her left. They didn't follow the normal stride pattern of someone walking or running through the snow, but they carried on for a while into the distance. Cache moved along the path. Snow had shifted, and she noticed she had moved from ground to a rock base, and the ability to gain traction would become difficult. She moved closer to the rocks and braced herself against them with each step. Cache stopped and once again cupped her hands to her mouth and yelled out for Angelo. She stood there and tried not to make a sound and listened for a response. Cache thought she heard something faint in the distance, but the sound disappeared.

Cache called again but heard no response. She continued along the path, seeing a large patch of rock cleared of snow, like someone had gone tobogganing down the mountainside. Cache could see the ground sloped downward, and with the thinner layer of snow melting from the sun that day, the rocks had become more slippery; she lost her footing more than once. She turned the corner to see a gray-haired figure wearing a dark blue jacket clutching at some rocks. His legs were not visible to her.

"Angelo?" she asked.

"I told you to go home," Angelo said, not looking up at her but facing down at the rocks.

"Just wanted to make sure you're okay, but you look like you're doing swell, have it all in hand, so I'll be going."

Angelo let out a big sigh. "I expect I busted my wrist."

"Which one?"

"The right one, but if I let go, I figure I'll end up going over this cliff."

"Can you hang on?"

"I don't know for how long. I've been out here for a while."

Cache pondered what could she do. She hadn't brought rope with her, as they'd never planned to climb up the mountain and would have let the helicopters explore that area if it had come to that. She could go back to the cabin and see if there was anything there—perhaps the bedsheets tied together would work—but she feared that by the time she got back he might have lost his grip. If the helicopter could get out this way, they might be able to lower a rope to him. She called Sam.

"Hey, I found Angelo, but he is in terrible shape."

"Can he walk?"

"Nah, he's kind of dangling off of a cliff."

"What?"

"I don't know how much longer he can hold on, where's the chopper?"

Sam was silent for a few seconds.

"Sam, you there?"

"Yeah, I checked with communications, it can be there in forty-five minutes. Can he hold on?"

"I don't expect he has the energy to wait. I'll have to improvise. Sam, I'll send you the coordinates; get the chopper here as soon as you can."

Cache checked her coordinates with her GPS app and texted them to Sam.

"Angelo, I need you to hold on as long as you can. I'll find something that I can reach out to you with."

"Okay, just don't be too long, I might tire of waiting around."

Cache pulled herself up along the slippery, rocky path, grabbing at the rock edges to pull herself forward. She dropped her backpack and rummaged inside for the saw knife she carried. Cache unfolded the blade, moved to the nearest pine trees, looked for branch sections about four feet long and sawed the branches free from the trees. She cleared any smaller branches from them, and those with some flexibility she put off to the side. Cache rummaged through her bag—how she wished she had packed some rope—and then she looked down at her hiking boots. Her boots were tall and covered her legs almost to her knees. From the top of them she pulled the drawstring used to keep the closure tight against the legs, to prevent any moisture from getting into the boots. Cache cut small sections of the laces and used them to fasten the sticks together to make one long stick of approximately ten feet or more in length. She then used the flexible branches as additional support and bent the branches around the bindings done with the laces. Cache pulled on the sections lashed together to make sure they would not break free and ran back to where she had left Angelo.

Getting back to him would be trickier now that she only had one hand to brace herself against the rocks while the other held the pole. She tried to figure out the best way to reach him. If she laid on her stomach and reached out, she might catch part of the slippery surface and plow right into him headfirst, sending them both off the cliff. She thought about holding one of the rocks' edges with one hand and extending the pole with her other, but she thought she might not have the strength to pull him up on top of the rocks with just one hand. As she weighed the different options in her head, she determined that the approach with the greatest chance for success was to lie on her back, dig the heels of her boots into the rocks and extend the pole downward to Angelo with two hands on it. The risk with this approach was that in order to pull Angelo up, she would need to bend forward first, and that could easily result in her tumbling down and going over the edge. As she approached him, she sat down on her ass and inched herself down into position. She found a section of rocks off to the side that she should be able to brace the tread of her boots against and pull Angelo to safety. As she inched down into position, rocks came loose and started to roll down the rocky slope.

"Hey, watch it, will you," Angelo said.

"Do you think this is easy? You've gotten yourself in a charming jam. If we don't get you out by sunset, I'm not sure how you'll manage through the night as the temperature drops."

"And if one of those rocks hits me, well then, it's over, isn't it? Did you call for the chopper?"

"Yes, I called Sam. The chopper was low on fuel and went back to the airport; even if they rush they may not be back for forty-five minutes. Can you hang on until then?"

"I don't think so. I buggered up my wrist, and the pain is throbbing."

"Okay, so let me get into position, and I will extend this down to you. I need you to grab hold and I will try to pull you up."

Angelo looked up at the large stick that Cache had fashioned. "What is that? Don't you have rope?"

"No, I can go look for some if you can hang on."

Angelo put his head down and thought; he didn't like his options. He had lost his grip a few times as he hung over the cliff, only to be held in place by his other hand. He didn't like his odds, but he didn't want to wait, and if this was his only option, then he would need to trust her.

"Okay, bring the stick down."

Cache anchored herself on her back, her left leg braced against a set of rocks jutting out from one side, her right heel dug in as best she could, and she leaned forward as far as she was able to with the wooden pole. It fell beside Angelo's shoulder, but he would need to grab it with his injured right hand while holding the rocky ledge with his left. He counted down out loud and then reached up to grab the pole with his right hand. It slipped as he applied all the pressure he could muster with his hand and let go of the edge, grabbing the pole with his left hand.

Cache ground her teeth as she pulled him forward, bringing his body up over the ledge by a foot. Angelo weighed north of two hundred pounds.

"Can you bring your leg up?" she asked.

He breathed heavily. "No, still not enough."

Cache reached down and pulled the wooden pole up hand over hand. Her arm muscles were on fire, but she knew if she gave even an inch, it would be over for Angelo. She screamed as she pulled the wooden pole up until she reached the last lace holding it together. Angelo's knees were now above the cliff, and he was able to dig his foot into the rocks and push himself forward until his entire body was on the rocky slope.

"Don't let go," Cache said, "you might fall back down."

She looked around her and thought out her options. The best bet was to bring Angelo parallel to her. She reached her left hand down to his right while she held the pole in her right hand.

"Grab my left hand and I'll pull you up beside me. When you get up here, I want you to roll over on your back and brace your foot against this rock formation." Cache pointed to the area she felt would give him the best support.

"I thought you said don't let go."

"Well, now I need you to let go and grab my hand."

Cache grabbed hold of Angelo's hand and pulled him up beside her as he flipped over on his back and lay against the rocky slope. He pushed his right foot against the rocks jutting out to stabilize himself. The two of them rested side by side.

"Now what?"

Cache turned her head behind her to look up the rocky path.

"If your wrist wasn't injured, I would say we climb up the rocks until we get to the top, but I think it's too risky; you might easily lose your balance and slide back down, and this time you might not be lucky enough to grab the rocks as you're going over."

"Then what, do we wait for a chopper?"

"I think it's our best bet. They can lower a harness that I should be able to get around you, and then they can take you back to the base. You'll need medical attention for your wrist."

He turned to Cache. "Thanks for coming and finding me. I thought I told you to go home."

"Didn't feel right leaving you out here by yourself."

"How did you find me?"

"Hannah told me you ran in a different direction from her and Regan was chasing you. She is romantically involved with Regan."

"You know, that bastard shot at me three times. Lucky for me he has poor aim. The first time I thought it was by accident; the second time I knew it wasn't. Did she tell you what the story is with them?"

"She shared how they met and how she thought they were in love. She implied that he planned the robberies. But I don't know how or why."

Angelo tilted his head back and looked up at the sky. He thought about everything that had gone on but still couldn't piece it together.

"Do you have her tied up somewhere?"

"Sam met me and took her off my hands. I told him not to let Regan anywhere near her; no telling what would happen to her if he got her alone. She's angry and confused. She didn't know he was a married cop."

Cache reached down into her pocket, grabbed her smartphone and called Sam. She told him she had pulled Angelo to safety, but they were in a rocky formation just above the cliff and Angelo was injured. She told him the chopper will need to bring a harness so they could pull

Angelo up to safety. She hung up the phone and put it back into her pocket.

"How well do you know Regan?" Cache asked.

"Not well enough; the detectives keep to themselves, separate from us uniformed officers," Angelo said.

"You said he was the detective that caught the Bolden brothers?"

"Yeah, him and his partner Williams."

"What happened to Williams?"

"He got promoted."

"But Regan didn't. Is that odd?"

"Williams is the one who was credited with the arrest, though he didn't have much more information than Regan, just at the right place at the right time."

"What do you mean?"

"He got an anonymous call. When the Bolden brothers went into their last bank, he rallied the troops and we were waiting for them when they came out."

"No idea who the caller was?"

"You would have to ask him. Based on the Boldens' history, I expected it to end like Bonnie and Clyde, with an intense gun battle, but Leo dropped to his knees and threw his gun away. Terry just stood there in shock. Leo convinced him not to give in to temptation. Had he raised that weapon and fired once, we would have dropped him in a heartbeat."

"So Regan's partner gets promoted, and he's stuck back in the detective department?"

"Pretty much, but it's not a big department, promotions don't come around a lot. So she said nothing about the Bolden brothers?"

"Shut down every time I brought up their names."

"Well, it's not like she didn't know them. She was dating Terry, used to visit the two of them in prison for a while.

So . . . she was sleeping with Terry when she was sleeping with Regan?"

"Sounds like it. He told her he was in computer sales and was out of town a lot. They would hook up whenever he got back into town."

"Was she from the area?"

"She worked at a truck stop in Wyoming on Interstate 80."

"Was there anyone else with them, another accomplice?"

"She didn't say."

"The only people that could have broken them out of the prison transport bus that we have encountered are her or the Fleming brothers, and the recorded conversation describes someone matching her description and not the Fleming brothers'."

"She would be looking at a triple homicide?"

"Or more if she killed Doug, Leo or Terry. She will be looking at a long time in prison."

"She shared her upbringing with me; rough. She'll survive, that's what she does," Cache said.

"My guess is with all the charges she would face, she might be cooperative in helping us sort this stuff out for any chance that it might reduce the time she'll spend in prison."

As they continued to talk about the case, Cache could hear the fluttering sounds of helicopter blades in the distance.

"Hey, looks like your ride is here," she said as she patted Angelo's chest.

Cache waved her hands in the air until the helicopter was overhead and lowered a safety harness. She grabbed the harness and pulled it toward her until there was slack in the line. Cache spotted someone leaning out the chopper door holding the line. She lifted Angelo up, put the harness around his back and secured it at the front.

"You're going up next," he said.

"Not my ride, this one is for you."

"Where are you going?"

"To get some answers."

"Leave him, we'll eventually find him."

Cache gave a thumbs-up to the lift operator, and they hoisted Angelo up into the air.

She heard him yelling at her that he meant it above the sound of the helicopter rotors, but as they pulled him into the chopper and the harness came back down for her, she waved it off, and they pulled the rigging back up and flew away.

Cache just lay back and looked up at the sky. Angelo was safe, and now there was one more person whom she needed to find. She rolled over onto her front and hauled herself upward along the downward-sloping rocks until she got to the top and grabbed her pack and her rifle. She took some extra cartridges out of her backpack and made sure she loaded her rifle, then tucked some bullets into her jacket pocket. Regan may have thought he stood a chance with Angelo; Cache was convinced he didn't stand a chance with her. The last anyone had seen, Regan was heading toward the Shellington cabin. Cache planned to return to the Henderson cabin to ensure that he hadn't found his way there and would sweep the area as best she could as she moved westward toward the Shellington lodge. Once the chopper had gotten Angelo to medical personnel, it would return to the area and also be looking for her target. She hoped to get to him before they did. She knew there was more to the story than met the eye. If it was Regan who had sought Hannah out, and if Angelo was right, how could one man exert so much influence over a woman that she'd commit multiple murders for him? Was love enough of a reason to put the rest of Hannah's life in jeopardy or was it the money? Cache had seen this before when she was in the military police; people who had grown up without love or affection would do anything for it, like a plant in search of water. Was that the reason Hannah had done what she did? Was Regan's love so important to her she would commit cold-blooded murder in service of it? She knew she would not get any answers from her; even after his betrayal, she still wanted to protect him. Regan, on the other hand, was a showboater; he enjoyed showing off, and Cache figured if she prodded him just the right way, he might show off for her.

10

CABIN NOISES

C ache examined the area around the Henderson cabin and found no sign of Regan. She continued westward, picking up the trail from where Sam had said he had left Regan as she headed toward the Shellington lodge. She took her rifle from her shoulder and held her finger around the trigger. All along the path there was just snow and trees, but she spotted no wildlife, as if they sensed something bad was in the air and were opting to stay out of the area. As she approached the Shellington lodge, she surveyed the open area but saw no sign of Regan. As she listened, she could pick up the sound of something thrashing about inside the small lodge, like an animal stuck in a trap trying to get out. She worried that a bear had found its way into the cabin; with all the comings and goings over the past few days it was possible that someone had forgotten to shut the door tight.

Cache crept up to the cabin, being very careful, and placed her ear next to the door. The muffled sound of a human voice was coming from inside. She weighed her options: Should she call him outside? If he were smart, he wouldn't give up the cover, and he'd stand a better chance in a gunfight hunkered down inside. Burning him out was not an option for her, as Arthur would kick up a fuss if he learned she had burned his cabin to the ground. The better option might be to go in. As far as Cache was aware, he didn't know that she had found Hannah, or that she'd rescued Angelo from a perilous situation that Regan had put him in. She also didn't know all the facts, and he was still a police detective. She stood up and retreated about ten feet from the door to make her arrival appear more natural.

"Hey, Regan, are you in there? Regan, it's Cache."

He opened the door and walked outside. "Hey, what are you doing here? I thought Angelo sent you home."

"Yeah, I didn't feel right just leaving the two of you out here. Sam said you headed this way. Have you had any luck finding the redheaded woman?"

"No, she's given us the slip."

"Have you talked to Angelo?"

"No, I tried to call him but it just went to voice mail. But I figured he might have more experience than you in this environment and therefore you might want the extra help—no offense."

"Well come in then, don't stand out there, it's cold out."

Cache walked into the cabin and set her rifle down at the door. The cabin was a mess. Drawers had been turned inside out. He had pulled the bed from the bedroom, torn it apart. The bed frame lay against the wall, blocking the entrance to the small bedroom.

"I don't know if Arthur will appreciate his cabin being torn apart."

"I'm more concerned with murderers than housekeeping. He can send the department a bill for all I care." Cache walked away from the door and picked up a chair lying on the floor. She sat down and stretched her legs out. Regan picked up another chair he'd knocked over, put it about five feet away from her and sat down staring at her.

He pulled the table in closer to him. Regan wanted to ensure that Cache wasn't hiding something from view.

"So what's the plan?" she asked.

"Find the redhead. You haven't seen any sign of her at all?" Regan asked.

"Nothing."

Regan moved his head from side to side, looking at Cache.

"What?" she asked.

"I'm trying to figure out if you're lying to me."

"Why would I lie about finding a wanted person?"

Regan unzipped his jacket. "Man, is it getting hot in here. You look hot, maybe you should take something off to."

"And then what? You knocked the bed over, so we can't use that."

He looked back behind him. The bed frame's four metal legs faced him, along with various rusty springs making up the bottom of the bed.

"We would break it if we tried," he said.

He reached into his jacket, pulled out an automatic handgun with a silencer attached and put it down on his knee. Cache realized she had made a tactical blunder in trying to move things along. As they'd walked into the cabin, she'd noticed a bulge in the back of his pants, which she attributed to his service weapon; she had not counted on his having a second weapon.

"I think you have a thing for Angelo. Perhaps you have daddy issues. Maybe as he slept in the lower bunk last night, you wanted to be on top, just not the way you were."

"That's way off base."

"Maybe, but you two seem to get along, and that's why coming back out here and coming to find me makes little sense. I got the distinct impression that you didn't like me, you didn't like my advances, and yet here you are, alone with me. Doesn't add up." He looked at her as she moved around and caught sight of her handgun on her hip.

"No, don't even think about it, you're not that quick. I want you to reach over with your left hand and pull your handgun out by the grip and put it on the table. No sudden movements." He held up the gun with the silencer on it. "You know full well no one would hear the shot."

Cache did as he requested. "I don't understand why you're doing this."

"One talent I have had ever since I was a kid is being able to read people. It helped me in becoming a detective and in other aspects of my life. When I asked if you had seen the redheaded woman, you were lying."

He placed his gun down on the table, grabbed Cache's M9, removed the clip and chucked away the bullet in the chamber. He then tossed her gun in the corner, picked his back up and pointed it at her.

She looked at him, tilting her head from side to side. "You know, you might be better looking without the beard. How long have you had it?"

He stood up, keeping the gun pointed at Cache, and moved to the door and picked up her rifle; Regan opened the door and, seizing the top of the barrel, threw it as far as he could, dropping it deep into the snow. He looked back at her and smiled. "Very astute of you."

"I try to please."

"How long have you known?"

"Not long. It was something Hannah said that got the

wheels spinning for me. If she says the same thing to the detectives handling the case, it won't be long before they figure it out."

"Not likely. Most of my colleagues are idiots; they won't believe one of their own was this brilliant. But that leaves me in a predicament. I can't have you going back and telling your story. Can I presume Hannah is back at the command post?"

"Sam and the national guardsmen came to pick her up from me. If it makes you feel any better, I think she still loves you."

"She was a means to an end. I always knew I would have to kill her, I just figured I would be able to make it look like she was evading arrest. All in all, she killed those two corrections guards—hell, they might even give me a medal for putting a bullet in her head. But what about you?"

Cache leaned forward. "What do you want to do with me? I mean, what do you really want to do to me? What is that deep fantasy you've been thinking about since we met?"

He looked over his shoulder at the metal bed thrown against the wall.

"If that's what you want, I'm game. I mean, there are worse ways of going out of this world."

He looked down at his lap, and Cache could see that he was getting aroused at the idea.

"You know, I could look after that for you."

He held up the gun and told her to take her jacket off, which she complied with. Then he told her to remove her fleece so he could see her in a skintight turtleneck. Her bra was absent, which created a distraction, forcing his eyes to focus on her well-endowed chest.

"See something you like?"

"You get over here, down on your knees." He motioned to her with the end of the gun.

Cache looked at him, smirked and grabbed the table, shoving it into his stomach and knocking the gun from his hand. She jumped up on the balls of her feet as he stood up and dropped his jacket to the floor, kicking it to the side.

"Oh, you want to play, don't you?"

"Call it foreplay."

He reached around behind him and pulled out his service weapon, pointing it at her. "Looks like you lose," he said.

Cache spun around on her left foot and knocked the gun from his hand as her right foot made contact with it. "I prefer a fair fight," she said.

Regan threw a punch at Cache's head. Her adrenaline was pumping, but she focused on her breathing, deep breaths to help regulate her adrenaline levels. She moved to the side as his punch caught air. She grabbed the front of his shirt and drove her knee up into his rib cage. He fell backward against the metal bed, and one of the rusty steel springs dug deep into his skin. He screamed in pain. Cache backed up to provide enough distance between the two of them in the small room. He threw a punch with the other hand; Cache was able to duck underneath his swing and punched the inside of his ribs on the other side with her palm. He grabbed his ribs. She could tell she had made effective contact.

"You stupid little bitch," he said.

"Want to give up?" she asked.

He took a boxer's stance and put his fists up in front of his face. "Not to you." Regan threw his third punch, contacting Cache's shoulder, and as she turned, absorbing the blow, he punched her in her breasts, causing her to fall backward and land against the door frame to the kitchen. He looked around the room for the gun with the silencer and spotted it down by the bed's metal leg. Regan ran to the gun and grabbed it as Cache jumped on his back and reached her arm around his neck, so his neck was in the wedge of her elbow. She squeezed with all her might, her chest throbbing with pain. His hand moved up with the gun within his grip and he pulled the trigger. Cache could hear the silenced gun go off. As she pulled back on him with all her might, she could hear the thud as the gun dropped from his hand. He reached behind him, grabbed her hair and threw her over him, sending her crashing through the small wooden table.

"You fucking bitch, why didn't you just mind your own goddamn business?" he said as he bent over holding his ribs and trying to catch his breath.

Cache rolled over on her side and felt the pain moving from her chest to her back. She looked at him and spotted where the gun had fallen to. It was closer to him than it was to her. She knew she could make a leap for it but didn't like her chances. She watched his eyes as they went back and forth from her to the gun and then back to her. After a few minutes of surveying the situation, he grabbed for the gun. Cache got up on her feet and pushed off running for the door. She got outside the cabin into the snow and fled to the side of the house, peering around the corner, waiting for him to emerge.

He walked out into the snow. "You think you'll fare better out here? I can just lock the door and wait for you to freeze to death." The lateness of the day was on her as the sky had lost some of its light. Cache crept around the cabin, looking for something that she might use to hit him with.

"Cache, come back in and I will put you to good use," he yelled.

She thought, In your dreams, but her jacket had her cell phone, and she shivered. If only I had my gun. Cache then realized her rifle was out here somewhere, most likely in front of the cabin. She moved to the side and looked at the snow. There were footprints all around the cabin, and twenty feet from the front of the door, there was something that had come crashing down into the snow. She peered around the corner as he seemed to look from side to side. Cache thought it was now or never, and she ran toward the crumpled snow, diving just before it. He saw her on the move and aimed at her; holding the grip with two hands, he squeezed the trigger twice, and as he heard the sound of the muffled gunfire a third, louder shot drowned out the other two. Regan felt his right leg become warm; as he looked down, he could see blood running down his pant leg. Cache pulled back on the lever of the rifle and fired again. The shot into his left leg brought him crashing down in the doorway. She pulled back on the lever again, the rifle nestled into her shoulder.

"Drop it. I was aiming for your legs; the next one goes through your head."

"Do it, at least I'll get some peace."

She threatened him again as she walked closer, aiming the rifle at his head. She could tell he was in significant pain, blood staining the snow in front of him. As she got closer to him, she flipped the rifle around and smashed the stock into his forehead, knocking him backward and out cold. She walked over and checked his pulse, then went to her back-pack for a first-aid kit to attend to his wounds as best as she could until he was able to get medical attention. Cache grabbed the pistol from his hand, then walked back into the cabin to locate his service weapon and the clip to her gun, which she reloaded and slid back into her belt. She dragged him back into the cabin, pulled out the remaining pair of handcuffs she had in her bag and cuffed his hands behind him.

She grabbed a chair and laid her rifle down on top of it, along with Regan's two guns, and grabbed her cell phone from her jacket.

"Sam, I got him."

"Is he alive?"

"Somewhat. Can you send the helicopter and get us out of here? We're up at the Shellington cabin."

"Yeah, we'll get that up there. Angelo filled us in on some details and Hannah has been opening up to the investigators, so we have a good idea of what was going on. Do you have a gun on him? Turns out he's slimy."

"No, he's in handcuffs with two bullet wounds in his legs and a nasty bruise to the forehead."

"How are you?"

"Starting to feel pretty sore, just want to go home and sit in a hot tub for a month."

After twenty-five minutes had passed, Regan came to. His first demand for Cache was that she take the handcuffs off; after all, he was a police detective. It angered him when she had to confess that while she had the handcuffs, she'd never gotten the keys, so she wasn't sure how they were coming off. As he tried to make his case that this was just a big misunderstanding and that they had gotten off on the wrong foot, the sound of a helicopter grew louder and louder until Cache noticed the snow being tossed into the air as the bird landed in the area in front of the cabin. Sam had come along for the ride, along with two other police officers who put Regan onto a stretcher and tied him down for the ride back to the base. Sam took possession of the guns, and Cache shut the door behind her before she made her way onto the helicopter and they flew back to the base.

The next several hours involved Cache's answering a multitude of questions from police investigators assigned to the case. They wanted to know what information Regan and Hannah had shared with her and would go from Hannah back to Cache to see if Cache could confirm that she had been told the same story. They told her that Regan had been transported to the local hospital in Hart and would be under police guard until investigators could meet with him to get his account of the events. At about three a.m., Cache departed the command post. It had been a weary few hours sitting on a cold metal chair as investigators tried to document every detail of her capture of Hannah O'Conner and Regan Fox, and the rescue of Angelo Malone. While the surroundings felt familiar to her from her days as an investigator, she had usually been the one doing the questioning.

The news had somehow gotten out, and with the storm ending, local and national reporters had descended on the area to learn what had happened to the murdered corrections officers and the escaped prisoners. As Cache drove her truck past the barricades set up by the police, reporters pounced on her truck, holding microphones up to the closed windows, and a cameraman stood in the truck's path, trying to get a photo of its occupant. The police tried to pull the reporters back long enough for Cache to make her getaway and head for the sanctuary of the Iron and Sons ranch. As she drove along Interstate 90, she turned the radio down so there was only the faint sound of a Tim McGraw song playing in the background. The quietness of the truck cab gave her time to reflect on the events of the past few days and helped her prepare for the barrage of questions that she would face from her family as they tried to reconcile what they'd heard in local media and what they were hearing from someone who had lived through it. Detective Merjon had asked Cache not to say anything to anybody until the matter was sorted out and they had filed all relevant charges.

The storm was now behind her. There wasn't a flake in the air. A full moon cascaded its light across the snow-covered fields as she passed them. Her truck lights revealed a plowed highway providing her with an uninterrupted drive home. How she longed for a hot bath and quiet, and then to crawl into her own bed and tune out the rest of the world for a day or so. As she approached the ranch in the wee hours of the morning, she expected it to be dark, but it was alive with bustle. The main house appeared well lit and lights were on in the barn. The trucks and cars of family and friends were parked out front, and Cache knew that it would be some time before they allowed her the peace she wanted and the hot water in her tub.

11

A SWEET ADMIRER

Two weeks had passed since Cache had fought for her life in the backcountry just south of Saugeen Mountain. Life had returned somewhat to normal as her brothers and she worked to repair damage to the fencing surrounding the ranch inflicted by the storm. Her mother and father had been fielding questions from friends calling to see if they could learn what had happened up there. The commanding officers for the Quinn Police Department and Hart Police Department had held multiple press briefings, which were reported on by local media and appeared as brief segments in the national television news programs. Cache had received a text that morning from Angelo, who had asked if they could meet up that afternoon at Maybeline's, a diner in Hart. He wanted to thank her and bring her up to speed on the developments in the case.

She arrived at two p.m. sharp. Maybeline's was a popular diner, but by midafternoon it quieted down and the staff would start preparing for the dinner crowd. Angelo was sitting in a back booth as she walked in. They'd decorated the diner in a red and white theme, with red and white leather booths lining the window side so that people could look out as they ate and people could see those they recognized inside the diner.

As Cache strolled into the diner, Josephine walked up to her to give her a hug.

"I called your mom, just to tell her we were thinking of you."

Cache replied, "I appreciate it, everyone has been very supportive."

"I think that gray-haired gentleman in the back booth is for you. You wouldn't know if he's single, would you?"

"Think he's divorced."

"Good to know. What can I bring you?"

"Coffee and a piece of your apple pie if you still have any."

"Always a piece for you, honey."

Cache walked to the back of the diner and took a seat opposite Angelo. Tape wrapped around his right wrist extended around the thumb and up under his shirt cuff. Josephine brought Cache a cup of coffee and a slice of pie and hung around for a few minutes to chat until she took a cue that they wanted some privacy.

"How are you?" she asked.

"Alive, thanks to you." He held up his wrist. "Doctors say I have to take it easy, it will be a few weeks before it's back to normal. Luckily there were no breaks."

"Hold off on your manhunts for a while."

Angelo poured some more cream into his coffee and stirred it with a spoon. "No more manhunts for me. The brass has agreed to put me on desk duty for the next few months until I officially retire, and that suits me just fine.

"We learned a lot over the past week, and I thought given everything you did out there that you at least should know the complete story, but you are not to repeat this to anyone until after this goes to trial."

"No, understood. Is this where you're going to tell me that Regan was actually Terry and Leo's brother, Ethan?"

The news that she'd realized that came as a bit of a shock, and Angelo spit out some of his coffee, then had to wipe the mess up.

"How on earth did you learn that? We just found out a few days ago."

"It was something Hannah said."

"She told you Regan was Terry's brother, and you didn't want to share that with us?"

"I tried to talk to your lead investigator, but he made it clear he didn't want to hear theories from an amateur and just wanted me to answer his questions. You know, he kind of pissed me off."

"Yeah, he can be that way, but you could have told me."

Cache took a bite of her pie and smiled as she chewed it. "It surprised me that a police department would not already be aware of that fact."

"We were, or our human resources department was. Regan changed his name legally when he was twenty-three to escape any association with his family; he wanted a new life. His childhood was rough. Dad in and out of jail, mom an alcoholic and his brother Terry enjoyed making his life hell. But most of all he never forgot what happened to Nancy. So from the HR point of view, it was private and didn't appear to affect his job at all. So how did you figure it out?"

"When I was leaning over Terry's body, I closed his

eyelids. I noticed he had the most piercing blue eyes. Now, there are many people with blue eyes, but his were different, almost ice-cold, and yet I thought I had seen them somewhere before. Then when I saw the dead body of Leo Bolden, I noticed he had hazel brown eyes but a cleft in his chin."

"Okay, I'm not following you."

"You see, when I was talking with Hannah, she refused to talk about the Bolden brothers, probably for fear that it would come back to bite her, but she was more than happy to talk about her relationship with Michael, Regan, Ethan or whatever he wants to call himself." She stopped to take a sip of coffee, and Angelo motioned to her to keep going; she set her cup back down and wiped a dribble of coffee from the side of her mouth, then she pointed at her chin. "She told me when Regan and she first met, he was clean shaven, and she preferred it that way because he had this beautiful cleft in his chin that used to turn her on. And then it hit me that Regan also had those same ice-blue eyes. That seemed like too big a coincidence."

"We talked to Hannah for a while. At first she didn't want to say much and had a lawyer with her, but then, when she heard she would be charged with all the murders, she seemed more cooperative."

"What did she tell you?"

"Well, for starters, it was Regan that found out his brothers were being moved from the prison in Quinn to the state penitentiary. He was the one who got the car for Hannah that she used for the getaway, and he concocted the plan to break them out. He knew the corrections officers would stop if they saw an attractive young woman stuck at the side of the road during a storm."

"Still, to shoot two people is not a simple thing to do."

"Regan took her to shooting ranges on some of their dates, told her she needed to get a gun to protect herself, living alone in a motor home. Told her what gun to buy, and he got ahold of a silencer for the weapon through contacts he had on the street. We think she might have killed one of her mother's boyfriends. We're looking into it."

"Based on what she told me about growing up, it sounds like he might have deserved it," Cache said.

"Maybe, but those corrections officers didn't."

"This was all over the money the Bolden brothers had stolen?"

"Yep. Not once during the time she dated Terry, or even after they were sentenced, did they tell her where the money was. I suspect Regan started getting desperate to put his hands on the money, because from what she told us, the whole thing was his plan."

"You mean the robberies?"

"I mean everything. He had busted a hacker years earlier and let him off knowing that the guy owed him one, so he had him run the pictures that the Bolden brothers had taken from the banks against various websites to find matches. Regan then passed that info on to Hannah, who shared it with Terry. The guy set up the fake security website and fake phone number. I mean, he did a superb job.

"According to Hannah, Regan had noticed that there were several older single women working in the bank. He wore one of those spy gadgets into a bank once and had his friend run a check against various websites to see if any of the women had expressed that they were looking for love. He found a few matches and the plan was in motion."

"So why bring his brothers in on it and why not tell them it was his idea? Why use Hannah?"

"He wanted to keep his distance. He'd had a significant falling out with his brothers years ago, hated his brother Terry for what had happened between Nancy and him and wanted payback. He told Hannah that he used to associate with some guys from his old neighborhood that would be perfect stooges, but he needed her help to control them."

"And in return?"

"And in return, they would get the money and run off and live a happy life together, while his brothers either rotted in jail or were shot dead evading the police. Never did his hands appear dirty."

"Still, during the investigation, would his brothers not have recognized him?"

"You would think, but when we looked into it, his partner Williams conducted the interviews. When it came time for the trials, Williams testified, Williams got the glory and the promotion. I always figured Regan was bitter about the whole thing, but he wasn't. He would get the money and the girl if he wanted her."

Cache sat back in the booth to digest the information that Angelo had shared with her. Kate Barnshaw and her daughter were walking by the diner outside, caught sight of Cache and waved, and she returned the wave. "Small town. Okay, so we recognize that Hannah killed the corrections officers and Regan planned the breakout. We know that they broke them out because they would never give up where the money was located, correct?"

"Correct. When Regan started getting desperate a few months back, he sent Hannah into the prison, and she told Terry it was over and she had found someone new. Regan appreciated how his brother handled rejection. Even if he was in prison, he thought he would try to break out, then he would hook up with Hannah. She would convince him they needed the money to get away. Once she had it, she would tell Regan. She would let Regan know where they were. Regan would put out an alert to the patrol officers hoping his brothers were arrested on sight and if he was lucky they would be killed trying to escape."

"But they got caught breaking out of jail."

"Hannah said Regan was furious, couldn't even trust Terry to break out of jail correctly, so when he learned that his brothers were being transferred, he figured that he would need to break them out of jail if they were going to lead him to the money. It was timing that screwed them up. The warden was so eager to get them out of his hair that he transferred them during a snowstorm."

Josephine came by their table holding a pot of coffee to top them up and to see if they wanted anything more to eat. Cache convinced Angelo to try the pie, and they ordered two more slices, as there were still things that Cache had questions on.

"So do you have any idea what happened to Doug?"

"Thankfully, that video camera he was wearing had all the information that we needed."

"Was it Hannah that killed Doug?"

"No, it wasn't. She did not want to have a cop murder on her hands, and we think her lawyer will try to paint her as a victim under the control of a sinister mastermind."

"So did Regan kill Doug?"

"Yeah, but from the camera footage, he didn't want to. Doug was in the wrong place at the wrong time. When Doug caught up to him, the camera captured footage of Regan standing over Terry's body, putting two more slugs in him and saying, "Mom always loved me more." Doug came up behind him and called his name and he turned around aiming at Doug, saying he wished he hadn't heard that, and shot Doug point-blank in the head. There was no way he would miss his target."

Josephine came back holding two pieces of apple pie and a can of whipped cream in her apron. She asked Angelo if he wanted whipped cream with his pie but decided not to ask Cache and left, staring at him over her shoulder. "You have an admirer," Cache said. "So Regan killed Terry and Doug. Did he also kill Leo?"

"That looks like Hannah did it. Once she figured out where the money was, she saw him as a loose end."

"Which explains why Regan almost appeared emotional standing over Leo's body."

Angelo finished his pie and sipped his coffee for a few moments.

"I am surprised Regan didn't search the bodies," Cache said.

"From the camera footage, it looked like he panicked after killing Doug. He got out of the area as fast as he could. It wasn't part of his plan. Had he searched Doug's body he would have found the camera that was filming him."

"So Hannah had the list, or at least half of the list," Cache said. "The Fleming brothers stole it, not knowing what they were stealing, and Norm Fleming paid with his life. She knew Terry had the other half, and she didn't know Terry was dead or that we had the other half of the list. So if she had found him, knowing the cemetery they'd buried the money at, she could have come away with part of it."

"Now, you can't repeat that. Hannah has been more than cooperative, Regan not as much, and you could get called as a witness when the trial begins."

"The lead detective told me that when I was being debriefed." Cache took a sip of her coffee. "So, are you still heading to California?"

"Yeah, my time is up here. I'm ready for a new adventure."

"Do you think you'll miss this place?"

He reached over with his fork and took a piece of Cache's pie. "Just you."

THANK YOU

Thank you for reading!

Dear Reader,

I hope you enjoyed *Cold Iron*. I have to tell you that I really loved developing the character of Cache Iron. What's next for Cache? Well, be sure to stay tuned. Cache will be back next in the book *Hot Iron*.

I need to ask you a favor. If you are so inclined, I would love it if you would post a review of *Cold Iron*. Loved it, hated it - I would just love to hear your feedback. Reviews can be tough to come by these days, and you, the reader, have the power to make or break a book.

Thank you so much for reading Cold Iron and for spending time with me.

In gratitude,

Alex Blakely

ALSO BY ALEX BLAKELY

Cold Iron

Hot Iron

Iron Proof (expected publishing Summer 2021)

MONTHLY NEWSLETTER

Join Author's Notes

If you want to stay up to date on the latest work from author Alex Blakely, join his monthly newsletter called Author's Notes. There he will share with you behind the scenes info on his current and future books as well as things going on in his personal life.

You will get to see book covers before they are released to the public and get to download exclusive content created solely for subscribers.

To subscribe, go to: https://alexblakely.com/alex-blakelys-authors-notes/

ABOUT THE AUTHOR

Alex Blakely is a Canadian author who grew up loving works of fiction in the classic "who dunnit style." A university graduate in the study of economics, he spent a number of years working in the area of finance before embarking on his writing career. He lives with his family in a community, west of Toronto, Ontario.

facebook.com/AlexBlakelyBooks

twitter.com/alexblakelybook

instagram.com/alexblakelybooks

THE IRONHEADS

If you enjoyed this book consider joining our Facebook Group called The Ironheads to talk about all things about Cache Iron and future Books from Alex Blakely. To join go to: https://www.facebook.com/groups/theironheads

Made in the USA
Las Vegas, NV
09 April 2022

47053782R00090